ROBIN HOOD

"And i shall think my labour well
Bestowed to purpose good,
When't shall be said that i did tell
True tales of Robin Hood."

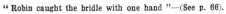
" Robin caught the bridle with one hand "—(See p. 66).

ROBIN HOOD
and His Life
in the Merry Greenwood

TOLD BY

ROSE YEATMAN WOOLF

ILLUSTRATED BY
HOWARD DAVIE
AND EDITED BY
CAPT. VREDENBURG

MAGNA CHILDREN'S CLASSICS

This edition published 1992
by Magna Books, Magna Road, Wigston,
Leicester, LE18 4ZH
Produced by the
Promotional Reprint Company Limited.

ISBN 1 85422 343 7

Printed in China

" He shall be King of Sherwood "—(See p. 12).

"Their true home was in the forest glades."—(See p. 29.)

CONTENTS

LIST OF COLOURED PLATES

" For very pity Robin stopped "—(See p. 50).

" Robin split the wand twice with his wonted skill "—(See p. 99).

THE STORY OF ROBIN HOOD

THE name of Robin Hood is a name to conjure with. It spells the Spirit of Adventure, and of great deeds. Round it for centuries ballads have been sung, plays have been acted, and stories written by the hundred.

It belongs to a vigorous and romantic age, to the time of Richard Cœur de Lion. To the days of the lance and knights in armour, to the bow and arrow, and the green jerkin.

It is a splendid story located in the great forest of Sherwood, where Robin Hood and his band of Outlaws roamed as wild and free as the wolves, the foxes, and the deer.

Such a tale of thrilling interest with its stirring episodes can never grow old, particularly when accompanied by the beautiful illustrations in the following pages.

E. V.

" Many humble folk blessed the outlaw's name "—(See p. 62).

"The outlaws rushed from their ambush"—(See p. 84).

ROBIN HOOD

AND HIS LIFE IN THE MERRY GREENWOOD

CHAPTER I

" It is a tale of Robin Hood,
　　Which i to you will tell ;
　　Which, being rightly understood,
　　I know will please you well."

MARTIN PARKER.

THE birds twittered and chirped in fussy eagerness to announce the dawn, for the pearly-grey sky was streaked with the crimson and gold of the rising sun. A bright-eyed squirrel ran down its grand staircase on the old oak trunk and shrewishly scolded a recumbent man stretched at the foot of the tree.

The slumberer, awakened by the shrill voice, stretched himself vigorously and turned over on his bed of leaves ; he lay there between sleep and awakening, and the memories of his childhood and youth passed through

his mind like a pageant in a dream.   He saw himself a tiny lad aiming
his first arrow, from a miniature bow, with trembling hands, and later a
stripling playing a bout at quarter-staff with his comrades, or shooting
at the target, and always his skill was greater than that of the others, who
willingly proclaimed him leader in all their sports.   Once more, by moon-
light or on keen frosty winter's morn, he galloped over hill and dale,
or chased the stag beneath the umbrageous growth of greenery and
waist-high bracken.

Then came the picture of a trysting-place where wild flowers spread
a multi-coloured carpet and the air was filled with the song of birds.   He
seemed to hear again the gentle plash, plash of a little brook and the shrilling
of a cricket in a thicket close at hand.   He stood there beside his true love
and plighted his troth to her, and sweet Lady Marian placing her hands
in his vowed to be faithful to him always, in sunshine and storm, in good
fortune or evil days, whatever might betide.   And always like a verdant
thread, connecting each dream-memory, ran the forest where he lay ;
for the glades of Sherwood had been his play-ground and his school, and
there was no bosket, by-way, short-cut or path however secret that he had
not explored.

In those days Sherwood Forest covered the greater part of Nottingham,
Derby and Yorkshire with a sea of shimmering greenery, and was connected
by many a path with another forest called Barnsdale, also in Yorkshire.
Until the coming of the Normans these had been the happy hunting grounds
of the stout Saxon gentry and yeomen who fared sumptuously on the deer
and game that abounded there.

Robert, Earl of Huntingdon, for the dreamer was none other than he,
roused himself, and sitting up reflected gloomily how all was now changed.
No more were the spoils of the forest the right of the people, no longer
might they enjoy the chase nor snare the game ; the bold man who

ventured to shoot within the pre-cincts of what were now royal preserves ran the risk of losing his ears, or even worse might befall him at the hands of the king's foresters.

Richard, the Lion Heart, far away in the Holy Land, recked little that his loyal English subjects were ground be-neath the iron

" I'll teach you manners "—(See p. 14).

heel of the Regent, John Lackland, and preyed upon by rapacious Norman barons. Not even to the Church could they turn for help and comfort ; the clergy being just as greedy and grasping as the rest of their Norman kin.

On the slightest pretext the well-to-do Saxons were deprived of land and money, and frequently their lives were also forfeited. The Earl of Hunting-don, Robert's father, was one of these sufferers who, after being despoiled of his property, was murdered at the instigation of the Sheriff of Nottingham. This sheriff, a base Saxon, nicknamed " Judas," persecuted his country-men with a view of currying favour with his superiors and advancing his own interests.   The Countess of Huntingdon, broken by grief, soon followed her husband to the grave, and Robert, orphaned and beggared, was declared an outlaw after seeking to avenge his father's death in an encounter with the sheriff and several of his followers.   Two men fell victims to his unerring aim, and Robert, obliged to flee to the forest to escape the consequences, sought refuge in its solitudes that were so well known to him.

At the time our story opens, Robert, heart-sore and weary, had passed his first night in the depths of the forest.   He sternly resolved to devote his life, as far as possible, to alleviating the miseries of his fellow-sufferers. Whilst considering how to set about this task he was interrupted by the approach of a number of his father's retainers, bold strong men, excellent shots and ever ready to wrestle, run or jump, as behoved the stout Saxon of that period.   They had come to offer their services to their young master, declaring it were better to be outlaws and spend their days with him, free and merry, than to occupy the proudest positions under their foes.   Robert gladly accepted their proposal to form a band of which each member would pledge himself to be true to the others.   With one accord they chose their young master as chief.   " Aye," cried they, " he shall be King of Sherwood, and let those beware who cross our path, for we will brook no interference."

Robert declared that he would no longer be called Earl of Huntingdon ; but as one of the brotherhood should henceforth be known amongst them as Robin Hood, a name simple and unpretentious as the new station, he was about to assume, demanded.

They now fell to discussing ways and means of living, and decided that the greenwood was their estate, and its paths and highways their hunting-ground, where rich travellers should be relieved of their overabundance of worldly goods.

" You shall rob the rich," commanded the newly elected king, " and give to the poor.   See that no woman or child comes to harm on our estate, and let the tiller of the ground, the yeoman and all who toil pass unmolested. The Norman and all clergymen of high degree, the greedy monks and the merchant with his bulging money-bags shall be your lawful prey.   Should a fat bishop or abbot come your way, bind him and beat him, for I much mislike their kind.   Kill none save in self-protection or in fair fight ; and above all keep in your mind the Sheriff of Nottingham and his foresters, for they are a traitorous crew.   Guests of high degree shall ever be welcome at our hospitable board, providing they bring with them the wherewithal to foot the bill.''

This proclamation was received with applause, and after having agreed upon a trysting place in the depths of the forest they arranged that should Robin ever find himself in danger he must wind his horn both loud and long, so that all within earshot could rally to his aid.

They procured suits of good Lincoln-green which rendered them almost invisible amidst the verdure of the trees, and each man was well armed with bow and arrows and a stout quarter-staff.   Very soon the exploits of Robin and his band became famed throughout the hamlets and towns in the vicinity of the forest, and travellers crossed themselves tremblingly when they entered a lonely path ; but the poor and needy blessed their names and remembered them in their prayers.

One day when Robin had walked ahead of his men he encountered a lusty fellow who might well have caused the bravest heart to quail, for he was quite seven feet high and at least an ell in the waist.   They chanced to meet on a long bridge that was too narrow to permit them to pass one another, and neither felt willing to make way.

" Go back," ordered Robin, " I wish to cross."

" Go back yourself," shouted the other, " and keep a civil tongue in your head."

" I'll teach you manners," said Robin hotly as he drew a broad arrow from his quiver and prepared to aim.

" Dare but to touch the string and I'll give you the finest basting you have ever had," the giant threatened.

Quoth Robin, " Just listen to the ass ; were I to bend my bow you would bray no more."

" Maybe I am an ass," responded the other, " but at any rate I am no coward and would not shoot an unarmed man."

" Nay," cried Robin, " you shall not call me coward ; " and throwing aside his bow he stepped into a thicket to procure a stout oak sapling. " Now," said he, " shall we fight this matter to a conclusion, and he who falls from the bridge shall admit himself vanquished."

Their good temper was quite restored by the prospect of a combat, and they fell to without delay. Some thwacking blows were exchanged ; Robin, though much smaller, was the more agile and succeeded in bringing his staff down on his opponent's body with such force that his bones seemed to ring.

" I would not die in your debt," said the giant, " so I must give you as good as you gave me." With this, such mighty blows fell that the very bridge trembled and the staves whistled through the air.

Bang ! thwack ! bang ! went the staves, and Robin, streaming with blood from a wound in his head, hit out and missed the mark. A well-directed blow from the stranger now sent Robin flying over the bridge into the brook below.

" Ho, ho, how fare you now ? " laughed the giant derisively. " I trust you are comfortable ? "

" Passably so," quoth Robin ; " I'm floating along with the tide ; 'tis somewhat damp, but cooling after the fray." He waded to the bank, pulled himself ashore by an overhanging branch and blew a mighty blast on his horn. Then approaching his adversary he held out his hand saying, " We have fought a good fight and you have won ; let us now be friends."

The giant grasped Robin's hand in a grip that well-nigh crushed it. " 'Twas a glorious bout," said he, " and I fain would have it all over again.'

At this moment a number of Robin's men, assembled by the bugle, came running to the spot. Foremost was a tiny fellow, lithe as a monkey known as Much the Miller's son.

" Good master ! what ails you ?   You are wet to the skin," he cried.

" 'Tis no matter," answered Robin, " this fine fellow has but dipped me in the brook."

The men stepped threateningly towards the stranger, and ere Robin could intervene he was laid upon by three of the men.   The giant hit out with such good purpose that the attackers were soon enjoying the delights of the brook, then laughing heartily he assisted Robin to fish them out.

" Well done ! "

"He assisted Robin to fish them out"—(See p. 15).

quoth Robin, " I would you were one of my merry men and wore my livery of Lincoln-green. Will you not join us, we have need of lusty fellows ? "

" With all my heart," replied the stranger ; " though I am a fugitive from justice, 'twas but to save my ears for the shooting of a doe. Never shall you have need to complain of the mettle of your servant John Little."

" John Little," chimed in the Miller's son, " surely if I be ' Much ' he should be ' More.' "

" Nay ! " cried one of the others, " by a simple transposition he is ' Little John,' which suits him as marvellously as ' Much ' becomes you."

" A christening ! " shouted the men in chorus, " let us make a feast to celebrate it ; hurrah for Little John ! "

Quoth Robin, " A happy thought, since he has baptised four of us, we can at least christen him in return ; but it shall be with choice red wine instead of water, for I would ever return good for evil ! "

Thus was Little John accepted a member of the merry band, and the appetising fumes of roasting venison soon filled the air, as a feast was prepared to celebrate the event.

CHAPTER II

" Her brother was Gamwel, of Great Gamwel-hall,
A noble house-keeper was he,
Ay, as ever broke bread in sweet Nottinghamshire,
And a 'squire of famous degree."

WINTER had come upon the forest. The gaunt branches showed bare and black against a leaden sky ; but a carpet of dazzling white covered the high-road, that led to Gamwell Hall, making soft-treading for the villagers whose voices and laughter mingled with the chimes of the Abbey bells.

" Come in and share our festive cheer "—(See p. 17).

The Hall stood isolated at the edge of Sherwood and was fenced in by an earthwork so massive as to resemble a fortress, and further safeguarded by a deep moat spanned by a drawbridge. Such precautions were necessary in those days when might was right, and a possible enemy lurked in every neighbour.

The villagers formed a circle before the house and raised their voices in " Good King Wenceslas " ; but before the first verse was brought to a somewhat discordant finish, the great oaken door was thrown open and the jovial face of Sir Guy Gamwell beamed upon them.

" A merry Christmas and a hearty welcome to all," he cried. " Come in and share our festive cheer."

The carollers trooped into the " Great Hall " (serving the treble purpose

B

of dining-room, kitchen and dormitory) and took their stand with the household retainers, close to the huge fire in the centre.

Roasting game, pork and venison filled the atmosphere with savoury odours and a hazy blue smoke that almost obscured Sir Guy and Lady Gamwell and their noisy party of guests. Foremost in the fun and frolic was their son Will, whose red head had earned him the nickname Scarlet.

" Now is your chance, Friar Tuck," he cried ; " there is Lady Marian standing beneath the mistletoe."

" 'Tis an occasion not to be missed," responded the monk, whose great height was matched by his exceeding corpulency, as he dexterously caught a young girl beneath the cluster of white berries, and kissed her.

" Fie, for shame ! " laughed Lady Marian ; " were my Robin here to defend me, he would baste you well for the liberty."

" I would the lad were here to do it ; have you seen aught of him lately ? " questioned the friar. Lady Marian's eyes filled with tears as she replied—" Father has forbidden us to meet ; he declares ' no beggarly bandit shall be his son-in-law ' ; it is very hard on us, for we love one another truly, and he also liked Robin when he was rich and had a title."

" 'Tis the way of the world, my child," said the friar, " to smile in company with good fortune, and turn your back on those upon whom the ' fickle jade ' elects to frown."

A bent old man now came in hesitatingly, and producing a harp from beneath his tattered cloak, looked anxiously at Sir Guy as though he feared being chased from the warmth and good cheer, to the wintry coldness out of doors.

" Welcome and a merry Yuletide, Master Harper," cried the host. " Play us a right lively air and you will not lack recompense."

The harper twanged the strings and raised a quavery voice quite at odds with the accompaniment.

"In faith," quoth Will, "I trust your appetite is better than your song, otherwise you will do scant justice to our good fare!"

"Aye, that it is," replied the old man with vigour, and rising suddenly he threw off his mantle and long white beard, and disclosed a manly form in doublet of Lincoln-green.

"'Tis Robin, Robin Hood," cried a chorus of voices, and never was there such a shaking of hands and slapping of backs; and Lady Marian, all rosy confusion, received a second kiss under the mistletoe.

"Here I am, Uncle Guy, I could not let Yuletide pass without greeting you all," said Robin, "more especially as a little red-robin whispered in my ear that Marian would be with you to-day, and you see he spoke true."

"To board, to board," shouted Sir Guy, "the roast will be done to cinders," and soon the long tables were filled by a merry crowd, one end of the Hall being reserved for the retainers and villagers.

The meal was bountiful and the wassail bowl made many rounds, to each of which the friar did ample justice. When the repast was finished Sir Guy called upon Friar Tuck to pronounce a blessing; but the good man was nodding in sleepy beatitude and heeded not. Will nudged him vigorously and whispered, "Wake up and sing a song." Thus aroused the friar rubbed his eyes and burst forth in stentorian tones—

> "For fasting and prayer
> But little I care.
> Yoicks! tally ho! boys, tally ho!"

"Truly a sweet air," said Will, "and must be in much favour with your Abbot"; but the sarcasm went unnoticed by the friar, who was again wrapped in slumber.

At this moment a travel-stained messenger came in hurriedly and, drawing Sir Guy aside, whispered in his ear. The colour fled from the old man's cheeks and he stood as one turned to stone. The company gathered

"'Tis an occasion not to be missed"—(See p. 18).

about him full of con-
cern as he cried—

"My friends, there
are evil tidings; I am
falsely attainted for
high treason, my
estates are forfeit and
I shall be cast into
prison."

"How know you
this?" Lady Gamwell
demanded of the mes-
senger, who replied—

"My master heard
rumours of it at Court,
and despatched me
post-haste to warn his
old friend, and on rid-
ing through Notting-
ham just now I was
informed that the sheriff had requisitioned two hundred of the Norman
rabble to accompany him hither."

Sir Guy still stood there muttering, "Attainted of treason, I, Sir Guy
of Gamwell, and King Richard's most loyal subject!"

"Aye, father," said Will bitterly, "to be loyal to Richard is no virtue
in the eye of Regent John; the traitorous rogue plays his own game and
Gamwell is a fat estate."

"Be it as it may," chimed in Robin, "there's no time for talk
or lamentation, we all stand by Sir Guy and will protect him with

our last drop of blood. We will make a good fight for it ; the sheriff and his rascals must have no easy victory here."

The guests were hastily despatched to their homes, and the womenfolk of the household set out, under escort, to the estate of Sir Guy's brother in Yorkshire, bearing with them as many valuables as they could carry. There were two score men now left for the defence, and they set about without delay to prepare for the coming fray. Robin had taken an opportunity to draw Lady Marian aside before her departure and bid her a loving good-bye.

" It may be long ere we meet again, but forget me not ; I will ever be true to you. Perchance when Richard returns, he will grant a pardon so that I may be free to claim you for my wife ; until then it behoves us to be loyal to your father's wish, however unjust his decree may seem."

They parted sadly but with brave hearts, for the sense of right-doing brings its own comfort.

Friar Tuck was not to be persuaded to return to his Abbey.

" Think you I am a rat to desert a sinking galley ? " he cried, tucking up his sleeves and swinging a great oak staff. " Ye will not find me backward when there are blows to give or take."

Feverish activity now prevailed ; arrows were made and placed ready for use, the drawbridge pulled up and the heavy door closed. Piles of dry fern and brushwood were placed upon the upper part of the earthwork, and skilled archers concealed amongst them, so that they were invisible from outside, but themselves obtained a wide prospect of the surrounding country. Preparations continued until far into the night when a halt was called and the toilers snatched a short repose ; but the wintry darkness had scarce dissolved into the murky red-streaked grey of early morn, when an outpost trod his cautious way over snow-filled ruts and ice-covered puddles

"'Tis Robin, Robin Hood"—(See p. 19).

to report that the sheriff and a large band a-horse and on foot were already within sight.

"Hurrah!" shouted the men, who dearly loved to fight those hated rivals who had given the Saxons so much cause for enmity, but their voices died into silence when they beheld the grief-drawn features of their beloved master.

"Friends," said he, "in this old Hall I first drew breath, and here had I hoped to die. It has been otherwise decreed, and naught remains but to sell it as dearly as we can; my heart would break were I obliged to fly without striking a blow in its defence."

"So say we all!" responded the men. "Hurrah for Sir Guy of Gamwell Hall! Hurrah!"

Each man now took his appointed station, whilst the sheriff cantered gaily along the road followed by his posse, which had been collected from the rabble of Nottingham. He was so certain of taking Sir Guy by surprise and thus avoiding any serious trouble, that he already reckoned on the favour he would receive from John as a reward for the successful undertaking. It was an unexpected check to find the drawbridge up, as it obliged him to remain on the highway instead of permitting the entry in force that he had anticipated. There was nothing for it but to stay where he was and, in accordance with custom, sound the trumpet, whilst in a loud voice the herald demanded the surrender of the body of Sir Guy Gamwell and all his goods and estates in the name of the Regent, Prince John.

The reply came short and sharp in the shape of a well-directed flight of arrows from the archers concealed in the brushwood.

Several horses, pierced by the shafts, reared and overthrew their riders; some galloped riderless away, causing dire confusion amongst those who stood behind. The Normans promptly discharged their arrows into the brushwood, doing no damage, as the earthwork afforded ample protection. The compliment was returned with such

"Tally ho! boys, tally ho!"—(See p. 19).

enthusiasm that the attackers, hastily gathering up their dead and wounded, about a dozen in all, removed themselves well out of range and held an anxious consultation. They now arranged themselves in groups that could dominate the Hall on all sides, and settled down with the intention of remaining at a safe distance and starving out their opponents.

The day wore on, both sides remained in a state of inactivity ; but hope beat high in the breasts of the besieged.

" It freezes hard," said Will, " by nightfall the moat will bear our weight, if we cross cautiously ; we can then make a sortie, and once at close quarters we shall not get the worst of it, I'll be bound."

The plan was eagerly assented to, and each man armed himself with axe or staff or any weapon in the use of which he was most proficient. As the short afternoon closed in, the Normans, numbed with the cold, laid aside their weapons to build comforting fires, and seated near the cheerful glow they were soon lost in the enjoyment of their evening meal. A number of men had been told off to keep sharp watch upon the drawbridge and sound the alarm should the besieged attempt to lower it.

" We have them like rats in a trap," laughed the sheriff, " for the vermin will not swim the moat on such a night as this, the marrow would freeze in their bones."

" What is it that looms through the mist hanging so low over the moat ? " cried one of the watchers, as shadowy, silent forms detach themselves from the blanket of moisture ; and then with the cry, " St. George for Merrie England," charge forward right and left with axe and staff and whirling lance.

The men, so lately seated in snug enjoyment, scatter like chaff before the wind and many fall, never to rise again. " It is the devil," shrieks one of the men as he flies from a giant form that strikes with an oaken flail, leaving a track of broken heads, and worse, behind.

" Nay, it is not the devil," chuckles Friar Tuck ; " but the heavy hand of Mother Church who corrects more in love than anger ; " but the Norman had fled as though the Prince of Darkness were indeed at his heels.

Robin meanwhile sought for his enemy the sheriff, who was nowhere to be found, for he had crawled into a thicket at the first alarm. He remained there safe from observation until he was able to join a party of stragglers with whom he travelled to Nottingham, where they arrived, frozen, starved and wretched, to the huge enjoyment of the populace.

When the defenders, flushed with victory, returned to head-quarters, they found that Will Scarlet and two of the men were missing. All the Normans, save the dead and wounded, having fled helter-skelter back towards Nottingham, torches were lighted and a search instituted for the three who had not returned. The men were found, sorely wounded ; but of Will there was never a trace, and at length, further search being useless, they went back to the Hall with hearts full of fear for the fate that might have befallen the lad whom they all loved. Fifteen wounded Normans were brought in and succoured, and thirty more lay cold and stiff beneath a shroud of snow.

" This is a hanging matter for us all," quoth Robin. " The respite will be short, ere an overwhelming force is dispatched to rout us out ; safety lies in the heart of good old Sherwood, so who's for the forest and a doublet of Lincoln-green ? "

The men responded eagerly, and it was soon arranged that the single men should join the band of " Merrie Men," whilst the married ones would dwell in huts on the borders of the forest, acting as outposts, scouts or messengers as occasion demanded.

" Marry, Robin ! " interpolated Friar Tuck. " I would fain dwell in the greenwood too, where there is neither penances nor fast days. The Abbey walls do cramp my very soul, and whilst the Abbot gobbles up the rich man's goose the friar must e'en be content with a half-starved cottage fowl."

" 'Tis well said," responded Robin heartily, " join us, good father, and in return for your prayers we shall grant you the privileges of your calling without its penalties. I warrant our green glades, sky-canopied, compare without detriment to your columned nave and raftered ceiling."

This matter having been satisfactorily dealt with, St. Mary's knew Friar Tuck no more, and his strong right arm was ever at Robin's service, though he also failed not to bend his knee in prayer.

Sir Guy, being too old for the hardships of the Forest life, was persuaded to fly to France where he had many friends, whereupon Robin undertook to leave no stone unturned to rescue Will, should he be in danger. The fate of the old Hall caused many an eye to fill with tears ; for sooner than permit the home of his ancestors to be desecrated by an usurper, Sir Guy had decided to reduce it to ashes.

The wounded having been removed to the village, and the building stripped of everything of use or value, Sir Guy with trembling hands applied the torch that started the conflagration, and when John's emissaries came, they found naught but a smouldering heap of cinders.

Robin, disguised as a palmer, journeyed to Nottingham in search of news of Will Scarlet. He learnt that the lad had been taken prisoner during the fray, and was lodged in a dungeon in Nottingham Castle. It had been proclaimed that on the morrow he would publicly be hanged on the gallows outside the city wall.

Not a moment was to be lost ; so Robin hastily summoned his men and bade some of them to assume disguises and mingling with the crowd on the morrow, keep a clear space open before the gallows. The others he ordered to conceal themselves amongst the bushes close by and be in readiness for his summons.

At the appointed hour the Castle gates were thrown open and Will came out guarded on every side. He glanced hopefully at the assembled crowd ; but seeing no likelihood of a rescue there, he begged a boon of the sheriff who had come in state to witness the hanging.

" I pray you," he pleaded, " let me not die like a dog on the gallows and disgrace an ancient name. Unbind me and let your men attack me with their swords until I lie dead on the ground."

The sheriff, however, refused this plea and ordered his men to proceed with the execution. At this moment Robin Hood sprang out from behind a bush and pushing forward to the scaffold cried, " Will, dear Will, take leave of me."

Before the sheriff and his varlets could interfere, he cut the prisoner's bonds and snatching a sword from one of the guards placed it in Will's hand.

" Defend yourself," said he, " there is help at hand ! "

Back to back stood the dauntless two, wielding their swords to such good purpose that the astonished guards ran hither and thither not knowing what

" The herald demanded the surrender of the body of Sir Guy Gamwell "—(See p. 23).

"St. George for Merrie England"—(See p. 24).

to do. All was confusion, for men in Lincoln-green darted from every bush and tree, shooting their arrows with deadly aim. The sheriff after one glance of fear and terror made away as fast as his legs could carry him, with his doughty men close at his heels, and they never stopped running until the gates of the Castle closed behind them.

"Stay, Master Sheriff, I would have a word with you!" shouted Robin after the retreating figure.; but the sheriff only ran the faster, and the mob who had turned out to see Will hanged, now cheered him and Robin lustily as they joined their band and departed unmolested to the forest.

CHAPTER III

"But fortune bearing these lovers a spight,
    That soon they were forced to part;
To the merry greenwood then went Robin Hood,
    With a sad and sorrowful heart."

Robin Hood and Maid Marian.

ROBIN and his men now formed quite a colony in the depths of Sherwood, and their haunts approached by short cuts or tortuous paths could only be found by the initiated. Under the shade of a fine group of trees, the men constructed a dwelling for their leader, who lived with Friar Tuck and his two captains, Little John and Will Scarlet. The lodge, built of rough-hewn oak wood, contained a large living-room on the ground floor and several sleeping apartments above. These rooms were at first somewhat scantily and roughly furnished; but grew in comfort and elegance as the wealth of the little community increased. The other members of the band found shelter in huts or caves in the vicinity of the main building; but their true home was in the forest glades, and they only dwelt indoors when driven to by the inclemencies of the weather.

One sweet morning in early spring, as Robin cantered through the Forest on his favourite horse, he found that, quite unconsciously, he had ridden in the direction of Trenton Castle; and its rugged outline, frowning above the swift-flowing river, soon came in sight. Trenton Castle had been forbidden ground to him since that sad day when, fortune no longer smiling, Baron Fitzwater, the father of his betrothed, declared that never should his Marian become an outlaw's bride.

Robin Hood now dared not enter the gates where as Earl of Huntingdon he had ever been a welcome and honoured guest; but he knew that the heart of his lady beat true to him, in spite of the caprice of the ambitious man who had sundered them. His love only burnt the brighter when ill-fortune blew its cold blast, and despite the baron's decree that he must no longer visit at the Castle, he felt drawn to approach close to the walls that formed the casket of what was to him the brightest jewel in all the world.

Whilst Robin gazed longingly at those grey stones, as though the vision could pierce through them, Lady Marian sat in her chamber within, bent over her tapestry. Her work made but little progress, for ever and anon the weird animals, and trees that never grew, were blotted from her sight by the tears that filled her eyes, and overflowing, coursed down her cheeks.

She was not much addicted to tears and repining, her bright and cheerful nature rather led her to look on the happiest side of things, even in that dull old castle where the motherless girl lacked all companionship suited to her years.

But that day the scent of the primroses in the bowl beside her, and the pleasant vernal sounds, birds courting, the bleating of baby-lambs, the call of the cuckoo, awakened memories of happy hours spent in the forest with Robin. She longed to see him again, as only those can yearn who have been long parted from one they love ; and feeling too restless to continue her work, put it aside and went out into the sunshine that sparkled joyously on the river.

She wandered aimlessly along the bank, deep in thought, until her reverie was disturbed by a voice calling her name. She looked around and beheld Robin coming towards her, his face alight with joy.

" Robin, is it really you ? " she cried, and for answer was enfolded tenderly in those strong arms.

" There are times when stolen pleasures are very sweet," said Robin at length, after he had satisfied her inquiries about himself.

" Yes," she returned smiling, " but like all thieves we must beware of being caught ; if father happened upon us he would scarce credit that the meeting was accidental."

Said Robin, " I have heard the palmers tell of sweet waters that spring up amidst the desolation of the desert, and I think this is some such oasis in our lives, and we could scarce refuse the refreshment that has been so unexpectedly offered us, it would savour of ingratitude to the fortune that designed it."

" Nevertheless, dear Robin, we must not tarry longer," replied the girl. " Perchance there are happier times in store for us ; till then, farewell."

By some malign chance, Baron Fitz-water chose this very moment to emerge from the Castle gate, followed by his page, Cedric. He caught sight of the couple on the river bank and recognized them as his daughter and Robin Hood, though they were some distance away.

"Dear Robin, we must not tarry longer"—(See p. 30).

He stepped along rapidly and came close to the lovers, who were too much engrossed in their leave-taking to be aware of his approach.

Like the bursting of a thundercloud his wrath poured upon the luckless pair, and he laughed to scorn their assurances that the rendezvous had not been prearranged.

"Knave!" cried he to Robin. "I shall take measures to stop all possibility of my orders being flouted again. The Castle dungeon is the place for you, until you are safely lodged in Nottingham."

He grasped Robin by the shoulder and led him towards the Castle, Lady

Marian and the page completing the melancholy little procession.   It would have been the simplest thing in the world for the outlaw to break away from the irate baron, who was no match for him in either strength or speed, but he would sooner have died a hundred shameful deaths than leave his beloved one to bear alone the brunt of her father's anger.

Lady Marian touched his arm and mutely entreated him to fly from danger ; but he heeded her not, and continued to walk quietly beside the baron, whose rage seemed to augment with each step he took.

" Ho there ! " he shouted, as they entered the keep, " put this villain in the dungeon and keep close guard over him."

Two men stepped forward at the baron's bidding and laid hold of Robin ; but their master reading compassion for the outlaw in their eyes, himself accompanied them to the cell and locking the door put the key in his wallet.

" Cedric," said Lady Marian to the page, as they stood waiting the baron's return, " try to find Robin Hood's men and tell them of his danger ; you are only a little boy, but you will do that for me, I know."

" You can reckon on me ; I would do anything to please you," the page assured her, " but it won't be no easy matter to find them in that big place," continued he, with great earnestness and a total disregard of grammar.

The baron having disposed of the chief culprit now turned upon his daughter and after bidding her hold her tongue and not answer him back, asked her what she had to say for herself ; and in the same breath ordered her to her own room and told her to lock the door and give Cedric the key to be brought to him.   Upon Marian pointing out the impossibility of complying with his request, the baron seized her by the shoulders and shaking her well, escorted her to her chamber and locked her in, placing the key to jingle against the other one in his wallet.   Although

"THE FIGHT BETWEEN ROBIN HOOD AND LITTLE JOHN."
(See Ch. I).

"WE ALL STAND BY SIR GUY!"
(See Ch. 2).

both victims were now completely in his power, he felt by no means appeased, and decided to carry out his threat to hand Robin over to the authorities at Nottingham. He set about inditing an epistle to the sheriff; but in those days writing was a little-known art, and the baron found himself immersed in a sea of difficulties. The perspiration poured down his face and he gave up the attempt in despair. There was none in the household who could aid him save Marian, and he knew he could hope for no assistance from her in this matter. He called Cedric to be off to Nottingham with a verbal message summoning the sheriff to come without delay to fetch the outlaw.

The page set off at his best pace, delighted at the opportunity to get so easily out of his master's sight, for he had not the slightest intention of carrying out the latter's orders. When well away from the Castle, he slackened his pace and pondered deeply as to how he should find Robin's men, the secret ways of Sherwood being quite unknown to him, so that he might wander for days and never find trace of those he sought. In this predicament his eye suddenly lighted upon the horse that Robin had left tethered near the river.

" Byrlady," said the page, " the very thing ; the beast will know its way home, I warrant," and mounting he left the reins slack so that the animal could follow its own devices. The wisdom of this course was soon apparent ; for the horse, eager for food, cantered along the paths that led to the heart of the forest, without requiring a guiding hand. Cedric found himself amongst a group of men in green, who anxiously demanded how he came to the master's horse. At his request they led him to the Lodge, where he placed the captains in possession of the story, and after a consultation between them, a plan of action was decided upon.

In compliance with their arrangements the friar was delegated to proceed to the Castle and make an attempt to rescue Robin from his duress.

C

The friar, being an old friend of the baron's and a general favourite with all his household, was considered the most likely to carry out the scheme successfully.

Never had the friar been more welcome at the Castle than when he arrived that evening just before dusk ; for the baron was feeling lonely and miserable. Not only did he miss Marian's bright chatter and kindly attentions, but the " still small voice within " was commencing to make itself heard, and he felt that in sending for the sheriff he had committed himself to a scurvy action that he now regretted. He received his visitor with great friendliness, and waiving aside the latter's explanation that he had just called in on his way home from a cottage in the neighbourhood, insisted upon his remaining to supper, and offered him a bed for the night, as travelling after dark was dangerous in those parts. The table was spread and the two men seated themselves.

" Where is Lady Marian ? " inquired the friar as he cut himself a generous slice of brawn.

" She sups in her own room to-night," replied the baron tartly, and hastened to change the subject, for he had no desire to confess his ill-considered and ungenerous behaviour of the morning, nor was his mood sufficiently chastened to make him desire to atone for it.

The friar ate and drank and in the intervals told such merry tales that the baron forgetting his troubles became quite hilarious, and feeling it his duty to keep pace with his guest, took a great deal more to drink than was usual with him. The friar, always a doughty drinker, seemed to have an insatiable thirst that night ; but he smiled to himself when he noted that the baron was nodding sleepily and failed to catch the point of some of his wittiest tales. " So far, so good," muttered the friar when the baron's head fell on his outspread arms and a snore was the sole reply to his remark.

Very gently the friar approached the slumberer and extracted the two keys which bulged out the latter's wallet. He tiptoed out of the room and made his way down the dark stairs that led to the dungeons. In the narrow passage outside the cells, two alert guards were keeping watch; but were quite satisfied to let the friar pass when he explained that the baron had entrusted him with the key so that he might shrive the prisoner, who would probably be hanged on the morrow.

"More's the pity, for Robin is a good fellow and deserves a better fate; but it would be more than our lives are worth to let him escape from here," said one of the men.

The friar opened the door just sufficiently to permit his stalwart frame to slip through, and disappeared into the darkness of the cell.

"Ohé there, you men," cried the friar from within, "where is the prisoner? I cannot see him."

"The beast will know its way home, I warrant"—(See p. 33)

" That is very strange," said the guards, rushing in hastily and leaving the door open whilst they endeavoured to pierce the gloom with their dim lanthorns.

The friar threw out his arms like a flail, and such was his strength, that the two men were felled simultaneously and lay stunned on the floor of the cell.

Robin stepped from behind the door and he and his rescuer slipped out, and turning the key locked the guards in, before they could recover their scattered wits.

Fleet as hares they ran along the passage, up the stairs and out into the courtyard without encountering any of the retainers, most of whom had already retired for the night.

" What about Marian ? " panted Robin as they came into the open.

" Leave the maid to me," replied the friar, " she will be safe in my keeping if only you can get away before there is a hue and cry after you ; stand in my shadow and mount the horse as soon as it is brought out ; I shall do the rest. " Bring me my horse," cried the friar, and as a sleepy attendant did his bidding, Robin sprang up with a bound and was away in the darkness before the lad had rubbed his eyes clear enough to see what had happened. The boy returned to his interrupted slumber, and the friar made his way back cautiously to Marian's chamber, the position of which he knew from the time when he had visited her there when she lay in her little wooden cradle.

" May I come in ? " he inquired. " 'Tis Friar Tuck, and I have the key."

Permission having been granted, he entered, and was warmly welcomed by the girl, whose untasted meal of bread and water still stood on the table.

" Did Father send you, and is Robin safe ? " she asked eagerly.

" Father did not send me," answered the friar, " and you need not worry about Robin, his friends will care for him. Your door is now open, come out, and I shall take you to some friends of mine where you can wait in safety till the storm blows over."

" My thanks for your pains, good friar," responded the girl. " I truly rejoice for dear Robin as I have been most anxious about him. I shall remain here until Father liberates me," she continued, " for I would not add to his displeasure to save myself inconvenience or even suffering. If only Robin is safe I can bear any punishment that may be inflicted upon me."

" 'Tis spoken like a brave and dutiful girl," said the friar, " and I venture to promise that you will soon be restored to the baron's favour, the storm was too violent to last long."

He took a kindly leave, and descended once more to the depths to release the guards, who were clamouring loudly for aid. Before letting them out he extracted a promise from them, enforced by all the pains and penalties of the Church, that they would never divulge how

" The baron forgetting his troubles became quite hilarious "—(See p. 34).

"The two men were felled simultaneously"—(See p. 36).

their prisoner had made his escape, to which they acquiesced the more readily as they were not quite clear as to what had really happened.

The baron still slept the sleep of the just, so Friar Tuck restored the keys to the wallet and disposed himself comfortably to await events.

Meanwhile the baron dreamt a dream. He thought himself to be in Nottingham, a spectator in the crowd that were witnessing the hanging of Robin Hood. Suddenly some one seized him from behind and hoisted him on the gallows in the place of the intended victim. Then a voice cried, "Death to the man who starved his daughter and betrayed her lover." He felt the rope about his neck and groaned so loudly that the friar, noting his discomfort, awakened him with a vigorous shake.

The baron sat up and rubbed his eyes. "I had a horrid dream," he said; "have I slept long?"

"A mere doze, a few moments at most," replied the friar mendaciously, having his private reasons for concealing the fact that his host had been asleep for an hour or more.

The baron's eye lighted on the remains of the meal that still stood on the table and his dream came vividly to his mind. " Poor Marian must be hungry," he said ; " perhaps I have been over-harsh with her."

" The fault is soon remedied," replied his guest ; " fetch her down, there's still plenty here to satisfy a hungry maid."

The baron needed no second bidding to go and make peace with his daughter, who received his shamefaced advances with her usual dutiful affection. She was soon seated at table and assiduously plied with the choicest viands he could find, by Friar Tuck, who managed to put away a few titbits himself, " just to encourage her," he said, although he had already supped most generously.

" I hope your mind is now at ease, Baron ? " inquired the friar with a twinkle in his eye, as he observed his host's gloomy countenance.

" No, it is not," snapped the other ; " Robin Hood is below in the dungeon, and I would he were anywhere else in the wide world."

" Let him out," suggested the friar ; " he'll take himself off fast enough, I doubt not."

" I dare not," returned the baron, " my temper is somewhat over hasty at times—not without reason," he added, glancing at his daughter, " and in the heat of anger I sent for the sheriff, who will now hold me responsible for the safeguarding of the outlaw."

" I beseech you, Father, release him whilst there is time," pleaded Marian, " and stand by the consequences."

" What, wench, wouldst sacrifice your father for your rascally lover ? " thundered the baron, growing red in the face.

Marian was spared the pain of replying to this sally, for the door was thrown violently open and Cedric came in, tattered and torn, and screwing a grimy fist into his eye. "An it please you, sir," he blubbered, "as I went on my way to Nottingham as you bade me, I was set upon by highwaymen, who beat me and tied me to a tree. I have but now escaped, so I could not fetch the sheriff, boo-hoo! boo-hoo!"

An expression of relief crossed the baron's face, and he dismissed the page with a blow of such unusual gentleness that the lad stopped his bellowing in sheer astonishment.

"To prove to you what a kind and lenient man I am," said the baron, feeling very magnanimous, "I shall release that fellow, under the condition that never again does he approach within five miles of this castle; if he fails to agree to this, he will be thrown into the river. There can then be no more trouble with him either way, and I shall have done my duty." He went off to perform his mission, kicking into wakefulness the guards who lay in the passage outside the dungeon.

"Here is the key, fetch the prisoner," said he.

The men entered and made a show of searching the cell, then rushing out they cried, "The prisoner is not there, he must have escaped by a miracle, for there is no possible egress from that dungeon."

"Idiots," bawled the baron, "there is a possible egress and that is the door, which you have failed to guard."

"You locked the door yourself and took the key," one of the men reminded him, "and there is no other that fits that lock."

This argument being unanswerable, the baron fell upon the guards and berated them for being idle, sleepy vagabonds, without the wit to guard a cat. Hard words break no bones, and the men secretly enjoyed the baron's discomfiture, as they shrewdly guessed how the friar gained possession of the key. The baron, returning to his daughter and guest, related that Robin had been mysteriously spirited away, despite the fact that not for one moment had the key been out of his own safe-keeping.

" The whole trouble was without doubt due to that brace of dunderheads who were sleeping when they should have watched," he explained ; " one can trust no one but oneself, it seems."

" Well," answered the friar, as he bid his friends good-night. " There are many strange happenings in the world, but most of them are due to our thinking a mote in our own eye is a beam in the orb of our neighbour, and acting accordingly."

CHAPTER IV

" But Robin Hood so gentle was,
And bore so brave a mind,
If any in distress did pass,
To them he was so kind."

THE next day Robin, feeling dull and depressed after the adventure that had so nearly ended disastrously for him, begged Little John and Will to bring in a guest to dinner.

" I care not whom," said he, " be it bishop, knight or squire, so long as he has the wherewithal to pay handsomely for his entertainment, only hasten on your errand, for the table is already spread."

After a while the captains returned leading a knight mounted on a sorry-looking nag. Robin noted that the rider seemed dejected, his hood was awry and his garments threadbare. The guest was courteously received and conducted to the dining-room where a well-spread table gave promise of bountiful fare. Friar Tuck, with eyes glued to a fine pasty, pronounced a hasty grace as the others seated themselves, the knight being ushered to the place of honour.

" I thank you for this kindness," he said ; " not having broken bread since dawn the prospect of so sumptuous a meal is welcome ; the more so since I learn that my host is Robin Hood, of whom the needy speak with reverence."

Robin acknowledged this speech suitably, and the meal was promptly served, with an abundance of white bread, red wine, fallow deer, roast swan and birds both large and small—to which they all did full justice.

"Gramercy," quoth the knight, " 'tis many a day since I have fared so well, I would I could recompense you for your hospitality."

"That is easily done," Robin replied, "for it would ill become a knight to dine at the expense of such humble folk as we are, and not offer to pay the reckoning."

The knight seemed greatly disconcerted at these words.

"It shames me to confess," he stammered, "that I have not the means to pay ; my coffers are empty save for a wretched half guinea." He appeared so troubled that there was no doubting the truth of his assertion.

"Do not distress yourself about such a trifle," said Robin ; "if you are in want, I would gladly assist you."

The knight, much touched by this unexpected kindness, thanked his host gratefully and prepared to take his leave.

"Stay," cried the outlaw, "and tell us how come you in your present plight ; have you gambled away your patrimony or lived riotously ? "

"You do me wrong in imputing my misfortunes to my folly," replied the knight. " I have ever lived quietly and temperately, and until a year ago there was no happier family in the kingdom than mine. Misfortune overtook us when my only son, who has since gone to the Holy Land, whilst fencing, accidentally slew a knight from Lancashire. The knight's family, desiring revenge, had my boy condemned to death. In order to purchase his pardon I was obliged to mortgage my estates to the Abbot of St. Mary's for £400. This amount falls due to-morrow ; but, try how I would, I have not yet been able to raise the money, so I am on my way to plead with the abbot to give me time. If he turns a deaf ear to my prayer, the estates will be forfeited and we shall be beggars."

" I know the Abbot of St. Mary's," Friar Tuck broke in, " you may as well expect comfort from a bed of nettles as mercy from him."

" I agree with you," said Robin, " it will not be easy to escape his greedy claws. If I lend you the money to pay the abbot, Sir Knight, would you promise to repay it on a date of your own choosing ? "

" By the blessed Virgin I do swear to refund every penny in a year from to-day," the knight promised eagerly.

" I ask no better security, Our Lady never has yet failed me," said Robin ; and he requested Little John to bring the amount, full value in gold, from the treasury.

Little John departed with alacrity and brought the gold which he had dealt out with a liberal hand, allowing five pounds extra in every score, for he considered it a charity to help a gentle knight who had fallen on evil days.

" Master," he whispered as he handed over the gold, " have you observed how worn is the poor man's clothing ? It would be seemly for him to have better

A knight mounted on a sorry-looking nag "—(See p. 41)

wear, and we have stores of merchandise from which a few yards would not be missed."

"Most true," acquiesced Robin, "give him three yards of each colour and every kind."

Little John wanted no second bidding; he measured each yard by his long bow and allowed one extra in every three.

"A fine draper you would make," laughed Will, who was standing by; "'tis easily seen you deal not with your own goods."

Little John paid no heed to the taunt, and when the cloth was rolled and bound he called Robin aside and suggested that a horse would be useful to carry home the treasure.

"He can have my grey palfrey, the one the fat bishop left behind when he dined under the greenwood tree. I would not be shabby to one who has given Our Lady for his bond," said Robin.

Will now came forward and shyly proffered a pair of boots to which Little John attached some fine gilt spurs, and begged the knight to accept this gift as a token of their sympathy.

The knight was quite overcome, and tears coursed down his cheeks as he embraced his new-found friends and started on his way.

"Farewell," shouted Robin, "we meet again this day twelvemonth."

"I shall not fail," responded the knight. "Sir Richard of the Lea has never yet broken his word."

On the following day the Abbot of St. Mary's sat at table with the prior and one of the king's justices who chanced to be his guest.

"It waxes late," said the abbot. "I misdoubt me Sir Richard of the Lea will bring the money in time"; to which the prior replied,

"I would sooner lose a hundred pounds than be harsh upon the knight, it would be too cruel to disinherit him for so small a sum."

"Hold your meddlesome tongue," cried the abbot angrily. "Heard

you not the justice re-
mark just now that we
stand within our legal
rights in seizing the lands
if the money be not paid
to-day?"

" He won't turn up,"
said the fat, bald-headed
cellarer who had just
come in, " he's either dead
or hanged, and there will
be £400 a year more to
spend at St. Mary's."

He had scarcely
spoken when the door
was thrown open and Sir
Richard of the Lea came in.
He saluted the company

"I am no false knight"—(See p. 46).

and falling on his knee, bade the company good day. The abbot did not return his greeting. " Have you brought the money? " he demanded curtly.

" Alas! not a penny of my own have I got," replied the knight.

" Then what do you here?" questioned the abbot by no means amiably.

" I came to plead for longer time in which to pay; it is but a question of
a few weeks' delay; as Heaven is merciful, I look to you for pity," replied
Sir Richard.

Quoth the abbot, " The time is up, you may ask mercy of Heaven an it
pleases you, you will get none from me."

" At least, promise to restore my lands when I settle my debt," insisted
the knight, who was still kneeling.

At this the abbot lost his temper and well-nigh choked himself with a piece of duck which he had just conveyed to his mouth.

"Get you gone, false knight!" he shouted. "The lands are mine, and mine they shall remain."

"I am no false knight," replied Sir Richard, springing to his feet and dashing a bag of gold upon the table. "Here is your money," he continued, "you sneak-thief, who would hide your villainies beneath the cloak of religion. Had you shown one spark of generosity I would have added a noble gift to the amount of my debt; but now not one penny extra will you have."

He strode out of the room leaving the abbot quite purple in the face with anger and mortification.

Sir Richard cantered briskly to Lea Castle where his wife awaited him anxiously.

"How is it with us, has the abbot been merciful?" she inquired.

"All is well," replied her husband, "no thanks to the abbot, but praise be to Heaven and our benefactor Robin Hood."

CHAPTER V

But Robin Hood, hee, himself had disguis'd,
And Marian was strangely attir'd,
That they prov'd foes, and so fell to blowes,
Whose vallour bold Robin admir'd.

"HE'S dead!" said Cedric, the page. "Dead as a door nail," assented the butler, "and 'tis but two hours agone that he kicked me because the sutler cheated him over the wine."

"Aye!" moaned Cedric, "and he pulled my ears because the kitten upset the milk, and now, there he lies and cares not a whit if the wine be sour as vinegar, or a dozen cats make havoc in the buttery."

" Just a stumble of his horse," interposed one of the guards, " and there he lay on the high-road and never moved again."

Thus suddenly was Baron Fitzwater summoned to another world, and Lady Marian left fatherless. The barrier that had stood between her betrothed and herself was removed, and when her father lay beside his wife in the churchyard, she determined to venture into the forest to seek Robin, for she was now alone in the world, save for some distant kinsfolk whom she scarcely knew. To avoid the perils that threatened a young girl travelling alone, she deemed it safer to assume the garb of a knight, and armed herself with a broad sword in the use of which she was proficient, thanks to Robin's instruction in earlier days.

Now it chanced that Robin had gone to Nottingham to make certain purchases, and in order to escape recognition there, he was so cleverly disguised as a beggar that even his own men failed to know him. As he hied homewards through Sherwood, he met a knight wandering in a lonely path that was one of the byways leading to the Lodge.

" Halt ! You cannot pass this way," he cried, brandishing his blade.

The knight, or rather the Lady Marian, who was muffled to the eyes, made no reply ; but being greatly alarmed drew her sword and prepared to defend herself.

Robin, noting that the knight was a mere stripling, slender as a reed did not desire to do him injury. He drew his weapon merely to frighten the youth from venturing further into the forest ; but the latter apprehending ill-treatment at the hands of the wild-looking beggar, made so impetuous an attack that Robin was obliged to defend himself. With the courage born of fear Lady Marian fought on, until a cut on he arm caused her to drop her sword.

The outlaw, always good-natured, picked up the weapon and complimented the stripling on his skill. Observing that blood was streaming

"'He's dead,' said Cedric, the page"—(See p. 46).

from the injured arm he set about to bind it up, and whilst engaged in this office of mercy, proposed to the knight that he should join his "merrie men."

"You might do worse than become one of us," said he, "and range the woods as free as a bird."

Lady Marian, who had been in a half-fainting condition from fear and the pain of the wound, now gathered her wits and looked closely at the speaker, whose voice rang strangely familiar.

"Heavens! 'tis you, my Robin," greeted the outlaw's astonished ears, and the knight throwing back the concealing hood disclosed the features of his beloved lady.

Oh! then there was a kissing and embracing; it quite scandalised a family of sparrows on a branch overhead, who twittered about it for days after. Robin blew his horn and the "merrie men" came skipping through the woods to learn what was afoot. Little John and Will ran ahead, and

"BACK TO BACK STOOD THE DAUNTLESS TWO."
(See Ch. 2).

"ROBIN HOOD AT THE MAY-DAY REVELS."
(See Ch. 8).

Friar Tuck was but a pace behind, when they stopped in amazement to behold their bold leader kneeling at the feet of a stripling knight.

"Comrades!" said Robin, quite unabashed, "I have found you a queen; I pray you do her homage."

When the situation had been explained to everybody's satisfaction, the men filed past and paid their respects with acclamation to the charming lady, who sat hand-in-hand with Robin on a grassy knoll. With great pomp and circumstance they conducted her to the cottage of a married retainer of the Gamwell family, whom she had known from her childhood, and where she could be comfortably housed until the time came for her nuptials. Friar Tuck pleaded to be allowed to marry the young couple out of hand; but Robin demurred, saying, "My lady and I must be wedded in church with due observance of the law. I have no fear but that we shall soon find means of so doing," he added, as he remarked that the friar looked doubtful.

"Halt! you cannot pass this way"—(See p. 47).

D

Never had men a gentler and yet withal a merrier queen, skilled in sport, as keen a shot as the outlaws themselves ; but always ready to help in sickness and soothe in sorrow. From thenceforward Lady Marian's presence was like a benediction in the forest-home, and those who had been rough and discourteous became gentle-mannered under her benign influence, whilst Robin showed himself even more kindly and liberal than heretofore.

Her title now seemed so out of place that she asked the men to call her " Maid Marian " instead of by her more dignified appellation, and by that name she was ever after known.

Shortly upon the events just narrated, Robin and Marian were strolling in the greenwood, when they passed a young man, who ever and anon picked a flower to add to a posy he carried and sang blithely as he went his way. A few days later they encountered him again ; but he no longer chanted his roundelay ; his head was bent and at every step he heaved a doleful sigh, so that for very pity Robin stopped and inquired the reason of his changed demeanour.

" Alas ! " sighed the young man, " I have lost the maid to whom I plighted my troth, and my heart is broken."

Robin and Maid Marian, full of sympathy, begged the stranger to relate the cause of his misfortune, so that they might offer him consolation and perchance assistance in his trouble.

" My name is Allen-a-Dale," he replied, " and the damsel who loves me truly, as I do her, is to be wedded to-morrow to Baron Podagra at Alfreton Church. The baron is old and ugly ; but because he is wealthy and I am poor, the maid's father forces her to become his wife," and the young man, overcome by his emotion, sat down on the wayside and wept.

Allen-a-Dale's recital suggested an idea to Robin's mind whereby he could do the distressed lover a good turn, and at the same time fulfil his own desire to marry Maid Marian in a church ; a privilege that in the ordinary way was denied to outlaws.

Plans were discussed and arrangements made, that resulted in Robin, disguised as a harper, travelling next day to Alfreton, where he entered the church and found the Bishop

"I pray you do her homage "—(See p. 49).

of Hereford, who was to officiate at the wedding, awaiting the bridal party. Presently the bridegroom, whose head was as bald as an egg, came limping up the nave on his gouty feet and stood beside the bishop, who with the abbot and clerk was listening enraptured to the sweet music the harper discoursed.

Robin laid aside his harp and approaching the altar demanded of their charity a largesse for the poor musician. The bridegroom shook his head, saying : " The bishop has an ear for music, I have none ; therefore he can pay for his enjoyment."

" Nay," said the bishop hurriedly, " since it is your wedding, all disbursements connected therewith fall upon you."

"'Nay,' said the Bishop hurriedly"—(See p. 51).

The dispute, which seemed likely to become a warm one, was interrupted by the arrival of the bride, who drooping like a broken lily was led to the altar by her grim, old, curmudgeon father. The poor girl shuddered as she stood beside the baron, and tears bedimmed her eyes, so that Robin's heart was filled with pity at her plight.

"This is not a fit match," he cried, "I forbid the banns."

"Begone, foolish man, your objections come too late, if you have any!" said the scandalised bishop as he commenced to read the service.

"Not so," replied Robin, "it's never too late to mend," and with that he pulled out a horn and gave three mighty blasts.

Before the sound had died away, four-and-twenty archers headed by Little John and Allen-a-Dale came rushing pell-mell into the church, to the alarm and consternation of the whole wedding party. Suddenly the bride beheld her lover Allen-a-Dale and fell joyfully into his outstretched arms, from which refuge she observed the crowd part to make way for another bride. This bride, even more beautiful and splendidly attired than herself, had entered on the arm of a tall and stalwart priest and now stood beside her at the altar.

"Proceed with the service, Sir Bishop, here is the true bridegroom," said Robin indicating Allen-a-Dale, "and I myself, with Lady Marian Fitz-water, desire nothing better than to be wedded in such good company."

The bishop flatly refused to obey the outlaw's behest, excusing himself that the banns had not been called three times in church, as the law demanded. Nothing daunted Robin ordered Little John to go into the choir and call the banns for both parties, twice three times for the bishop's satisfaction, and once more for luck. But the prelate was still dissatisfied. "Very well, then, Friar Tuck will officiate," quoth Robin, pushing the obdurate bishop aside and seizing the book.

Now the bishop was round and fat and as the push had not been a gentle one, he rolled over and over, bumping down the altar steps right on to the baron's gouty foot. Maddened by the pain the baron struck the bishop savagely, and the latter, picking himself up, retaliated with interest. An unseemly fight was soon in progress between the aggrieved parties, to the delight of Robin's men, who egged on first one and then the other of the combatants by scoffs and cheers. The abbot and clerk, amazed spectators, now intervened and separated the combatants, who continued to glare at one another like two angry cats.

Friar Tuck meanwhile, taking advantage of the altercation, slipped into the bishop's place and hastily performed the marriage ceremony for both couples, and this done they quickly left the church.

Allen-a-Dale's father-in-law and the disappointed bridegroom gazed after them powerless to interfere, for they were surrounded by archers with drawn bows, who remained at their stations until long after the bridal party had clattered away in a cloud of dust. Allen-a-Dale and his wife

"'Very well, then, Friar Tuck will officiate'"—(See p. 53).

accompanied Robin and his sweet bride to Sherwood, and gladly consented to remain at a cottage near the lodge, where they dwelt contentedly for many years, the two ladies, who shared recollections of so eventful a wedding day, becoming fast friends.

When the archers withdrew from the church they locked and barred the heavy door behind them, and as the windows were high and narrow, the prisoners could find no means of egress, until a passer-by, attracted by their cries, summoned aid and released the abject and tattered crew.

The bishop and Baron Podagra, making common cause, sullenly vowed vengeance on Robin Hood, and the abbot and clerk said Amen !

CHAPTER VI

" From wealthy abbots' chests and churls' abundant store,
What oftentimes he took, he shar'd amongst the poor."
DRAYTON.

 YEAR had elapsed since Sir Richard of the Lea paid his memorable visit to Sherwood Forest. As a result of careful husbandry and thrift he found himself possessed of a sum considerably over the £400 that he owed to Robin Hood, and he decided to expend this in gifts for his friends, the outlaws. He therefore purchased a hundred of the best bows that were to be obtained and a hundred quivers of the finest arrows, all bedecked with peacock's feathers and notched with silver, and then set out for the forest with an escort of a hundred mounted lancers in liveries of red and white. This imposing procession found difficulty in threading its way through the narrow streets of York, thronged as they were with people who had come out to witness a wrestling bout, which was held annually in the market place. Sir Richard stayed awhile to watch the sport, which was nearing a finish, when a stalwart Southerner came forward and challenged a great sinewy blacksmith to a further trial of skill.

The smith readily accepted the challenge, for having been a Country champion for several years in succession he feared no rival, and was quite certain of gaining the coveted first prize—a very fine horse. He came forward with a mocking smile, and was loudly cheered by his supporters ; but events soon proved that he had met his master.

Before the second round was finished, the smith sustained a back-fall and lay unconscious on the ground, and his backers looked glum, until one of their number shouted, " Out with the stranger, duck him in the river, put him in the stocks, we want no foreigners here ! " whereupon they fell upon the victor, and things would have gone badly with him had Sir Richard not intervened. With the assistance of his retinue he rescued the stranger from the infuriated Yorkshire men and saw him safely beyond the city walls.

" Thank me no thanks," said Sir Richard in reply to the Southerner's expressions of gratitude, " I could not stand by and witness an injustice because of the love I bear Robin Hood, the deliverer of the oppressed and the champion of fair play ! "

He pressed a gift of five marks upon the stranger and hurried off with his men, for he had tarried long on his way and had yet far to ride.

Robin awaited Sir Richard in the greenwood until long after noon-day and heeded not the solicitations of Marian to return home to dinner. He shook his head sorrowfully, saying, " I care not to eat, for I fear I have offended Our Lady. Never before has she failed me when I put my trust in her."

" I would stake my soul on her faith and the knight's honour. You will not be disappointed, mark my words," replied Little John.

" It may be," Robin answered, " but it is past the appointed hour already ; anyway, if we must eat, let us at least have a guest to bear us company and while away the time."

Little John applauded this decision and calling Will Scarlet and Much, set out on the errand without delay. When they came to the highway, they looked east and then they looked west, but not a soul was in sight. They were about to seek in another direction when they espied two black monks mounted on palfreys, followed by seven sumpter horses led by grooms, and behind these a long procession of serving men, coming from Barnsdale Forest.

" I'll be bound," quoth Little John, " that our good Robin will not lack company at dinner to-day. Get yourselves ready for the attack, my trusty comrades."

" There is a score of men at least, and we are but three," objected Much.

" Surely," responded Little John, " three of Robin Hood's merrie men are equal to twenty varlets such as these."

As the procession came near the three men stepped into the road with drawn bows, and Little John cried, " Halt ! if you value your lives ! "

The foremost monk pulled up, indeed he had but little choice in the matter, with those quivering arrows at such close quarters.

" Stir not, for your life lies in my hand," came the order from Little John, and the monk obeyed in fear and trembling.

" By what right do you bar the way ? " he demanded.

" I bear a message from my master, that he is wroth you should be late for dinner, when he desires your company," replied Little John.

" I think you make some mistake," said the other ; " who is your master ? "

" He is Robin Hood, and his will is law in this forest," boasted the former, but the monk broke in angrily—

" Your master is an infamous thief of whom I have never heard any good, and as to you, my fine fellow, we shall see whose will is law after my men have given you a good beating."

He turned to summon his retainers to make good his threat, but they had fled like one man at the first alarm, and no one was visible save a faithful groom and a little page who stood beside the sumpter horses. The outlaws grinned at the monk's evident discomfiture, and their spokesman indicated that enough valuable time had already been lost, and they must trouble their guest to accompany them without further parley, unless he felt a particular desire to have an arrow through his heart. What with fear and fury the monk could scarce sit on his saddle, but Will and Much held him firmly on, whilst Little John assisted the page and the groom to lead the seven horses. Robin stood at the Lodge door and received his guest with his customary politeness ; but the monk scowled sullenly and took no notice of him.

" Whence come you and whither bound ? " demanded Robin.

" I see no reason to answer your question," the monk retorted rudely.

"Nay, perhaps not," said the outlaw, "but I can find you an excellent one," and he blew a blast upon his horn.

At the sound, seven score brawny men in mantles of grey and scarlet appeared, as it were from nowhere, and formed in rows in front of their master and his visitor.

"'Halt! if you value your lives!'"—
(See p. 56).

(See p. 56).

"Take this churl and hang him to the nearest tree," he commanded, and was about to add some further directions when the monk fell trembling to his knees.

"Forgive me, kind sir," he implored, "and do not harm me ; I am the high cellarer at the Abbey of St. Mary, and I was travelling to London on important business for the Church. I prithee let me go without delay, and I shall intercede for you with our Blessed Virgin."

"Not so fast, my friend," said Robin, "and get up from your knees, for you are doubly welcome since I learn that you come from the Abbey of St. Mary. I doubt not Our Lady has sent you to repay the debt for which she was security."

He ordered his men to retire, saying that the monk's reply had been so satisfactory there could now be no question of hanging him, and he viewed with an approving eye the sumpter horses that Little John had just brought in.

" I know not of any bond Our Lady has with you," declared the cellarer, " and I am familiar with the contents of the Abbey ledgers."

" I fear you are no true servant of the Saint, as you profess, if she kept you in ignorance of the purpose of your journey when she sent you here ; it seems as though she did not altogether trust you," spoke Robin, and put a question which caused the cellarer to turn pale, for the demand was, " How much money have you in your saddle-bags ? "

" I have but twenty marks, upon my honour, just enough to carry me on my journey," vowed the monk.

" Good," said Robin, " if that be so, I shall not touch the money ; I would not take what you require for expenses—indeed if you are short I can lend you some—but if there be more than what you state, never a penny of it shall I leave."

The bags were unfastened from the horse, and a search instituted. Little John threw the contents into his outspread mantle and revealed to the astonished gaze of the bystanders a sum of £800 in gold.

" Master," he exclaimed, " Our Lady has not failed you, in her generosity she has sent just double the amount of her bond."

Robin's face beamed with satisfaction.

" I am truly rejoiced," said he, " not on account of the money, but because St. Mary has kept her faith with me ; and now let us to table, Sir Cellarer, we must drink a bumper of best red wine together in her honour."

The monk took the place assigned to him at table, but did scant justice to the generous fare, and glared with animosity at Friar Tuck, who,
fat and jolly as ever, indulged in many a sly quip at the expense of his
former associate at St. Mary's. When his uncomfortable meal was at
length finished, the cellarer rose, eager to depart, but Robin detained him
with a gesture, saying, " Not so fast, my friend ; before you go you must
settle your bill."

" That is impossible, since you have robbed me of every penny I had,"
the monk expostulated.

" I took naught that was yours," responded his host, " you acted
but as deputy in that matter of the debt, the money did not belong to
you."

He then called Little John and ordered him to take the sumpter horses
in payment of the cellarer's bill, adding that he felt sure the latter would
not care to go away owing money that he might feel it inconvenient to
bring at some other time.

" Faith," moaned the cellarer as he dug his spurs into his palfrey,
" I would have dined more cheaply and in better company at Blyth or
Doncaster, although the inns there are the dearest and worst in all
England."

The page and the groom had received better treatment than their
master, for after a good meal, Robin himself praised them for their
faithfulness to their trust, and presented them with twenty marks as a
reward.

After taking leave of these men, Robin walked to the great highway
where he noted a cloud of dust some distance off, and his sharp eye soon
detected Sir Richard of the Lea riding hard in the midst of it. He
hurried along to greet his friend, and Sir Richard seeing him approach,
alit from his horse crying, " God save you, good Robin Hood."

Robin bade the knight welcome and inquired how things had prospered since they last met.

"All is well with me and mine, thanks be to God and you," replied Sir Richard, who then apologised for having missed the hour of his appointment, and explained the cause of the delay at York.

When they came to the Lodge the newcomer was warmly greeted by all the company, including Marian, who had heard of his misfortunes.

"And now," said the knight, "it devolves upon me to settle my debt, and here is the £400, with twenty marks over for your courtesy."

"I thank you from my heart, but your debt has already been settled by Our Lady herself; she sent the high cellarer with the money; I could not shame myself by taking payment twice over," Robin declared.

"Nevertheless," said Sir Richard, "I have the money here and it is yours;" but Robin refused to accept it and related the tale of the monk amidst much merriment and laughter.

Great was the surprise and pleasure of the recipients when Sir Richard presented his gift of the bows and arrows—one and all declared that never

"A sum of £800 in gold"—(See p. 59).

had they seen such splendid workmanship, and were unanimous in their praise and thanks.

" It is but a trifle," said Sir Richard modestly, " and I hope that some day I shall have the opportunity of showing you greater kindness ; do not forget that in me you have a true friend."

They parted in good will and amity, amidst acclamations from all Robin's lusty men, their cheers ringing in Sir Richard's ears long after he had crossed the borders of the greenwood.

Robin made careful inquiries amongst the cottagers, and distributed the £800 taken from the monk, wherever there was poverty or sickness, so that many humble folk blessed the outlaw's name that winter.

"'I would have dined more cheaply and in better company at Blyth or Doncaster'"—(See p. 60).

" ' Where are you off to all in the wet?' "—(See p. 64).

CHAPTER VII

The sheriff he saddled his good palfréy,
And, with three hundred pounds in gold,
Away he went with bold Robin Hood,
His horned beasts to behold.—*Old Song*.

IT was the wettest and coldest part of the winter ; moisture dripped from every branch, the highways were a sea of mud, and the forest paths little better than quagmires. The merrie men sat in the warm shelter of their huts feeling disinclined to brave the keen nipping wind, Robin alone was too restless to remain indoors.

" I think I'll go to Nottingham and see what's doing there," he remarked to Marian, and despite her entreaties to remain at home and not risk unnecessary danger, he cleverly disguised his face, and wrapping a tattered mantle about him, set out cheerily on his way.

As he plodded along squelching mud at every step he met a jolly-looking butcher mounted on a grey mare.

"Good morrow," said Robin, "where are you off to all in the wet ? "

"To Nottingham market to sell my meat, worse luck ! I had rather sit by the fireside in such weather ; but one must live ! " answered the butcher.

"It must be a jolly life, nevertheless," said Robin ; "I should like to be a butcher ; perhaps we can make a bargain.   What is the price of your meat, basket and horse ? "

"Four marks," replied the butcher, "and cheap at the price ; but I would not be hard on a poor man," he added, glancing at the outlaw's ragged mantle.

"Done," said Robin, "and I would add another mark in exchange for your clothes, if you be willing."

The butcher gladly accepted the offer as the bargain was to his advantage, and tramped homewards wrapped in the old cloak.

Robin cantered gaily to Nottingham and made for the market-place which was thronged with buyers and sellers. He took his stand amongst the other butchers and commenced to cry his wares. A crowd soon gathered round him, the women eagerly pushing one another to get near, for he was selling the same quantity of meat for a penny as the others gave for five. The butchers scratched their heads and looked glum, for not one pound of meat could they sell that day, whilst Robin's stock decreased rapidly.

"Surely," said they to one another, "this must be some young prodigal dissipating his father's wealth, or else a thief disposing of stolen meat ; anyway we might try to make a bit out of him, as he seems so lavish with his money."

Robin had just disposed of his last piece of meat, a sheep's head, which

"ROBIN HOOD MEETS THE BISHOP OF HEREFORD."
(*See Ch. 8*).

"ROBIN HOOD RESCUES LITTLE JOHN."
(See Ch. 9).

he presented to a beldame for nothing, " as a suitable tribute to her beauty," he told her, amidst the laughter of the crowd, when one of the butchers came up and begged him to join his brother tradesmen at dinner.

" For sure," said Robin, " I shall come right gladly ; he who would deny so kind a request would indeed be a churl."

As it was customary on market days for the butchers to have their meals served in common—each man paying his own score—in a room at the sheriff's house, Robin found himself seated there at a long table as the guest of honour, to his secret amusement. The sheriff sat at the head of the table, encouraging his visitors to pass round the wine, which being a very inferior article at a high price, brought him in a handsome profit. The outlaw was the life and soul of the party.

" Eat, drink and be merry, my brothers," he cried, " for I shall pay the score."

" He is a mad fellow," whispered the butchers to one another ; but they filled their horns and drank his health in good-fellowship before they went their ways on somewhat unsteady legs.

The sheriff said little during the meal ; he ate and drank as much as he could and his thoughts were busy at the same time. He concluded that Robin was a foolish spendthrift, who had probably come into an inheritance and lacked the sense to husband it.

" My good fellow," he said, detaining Robin as he was about to take his leave, " stay awhile and drink a bumper of wine with me."

" With all my heart," the other acquiesced, seating himself again.

" I suppose you have quite a nice estate and some fine cattle," insinuated the sheriff.

" Yes, that I have, sir, a hundred acres of good land and at least five score of fat horned beasts," replied the supposed butcher.

E

"Would you be disposed to sell?" inquired the sheriff, anxious to drive a bargain to his own advantage with the simpleton who parted so readily with his money.

Before replying Robin considered a moment. "It is like this," he said, "I would not willingly part with such a good property, but as I am short of ready money, I am not averse to selling it at a low price if the gold is paid cash."

The sheriff's eyes twinkled greedily. "That is all very fine," he said, "but I am not going to buy a pig-in-a-poke."

"Certainly not; if the property pleases you after you have seen it, you can have it for £500," agreed Robin.

"Make it £300," cried the sheriff, "and I'll saddle my nag and come right away to view it."

This having been satisfactorily arranged, the sheriff stowed his £300 in gold securely in the saddle-bag, and they set out without delay. After they had journeyed some distance and the short winter afternoon was drawing to a close, the sheriff asked if they had much further to go.

"It is some distance yet," replied his guide; "we must cross part of the forest."

"Heaven keep that scamp Robin Hood out of our path," muttered the sheriff as they entered a lonely glade. A herd of magnificent deer loomed through the mist quite close to the travellers.

"Ah!" cried Robin, "here are my horned beasts, master sheriff; how like you them?"

The sheriff made no reply, but glanced suspiciously at his companion, and digging his spurs into his horse endeavoured to make off as fast as possible.

Robin caught the bridle with one hand, and with the other drew out his horn. As if by magic, at the first blast, the woodland was alive with green-clad figures who came running to their master.

" What are your orders ? " cried Will Scarlet as he came near.

" Here is a guest who has come to supper," said Robin, pointing to the trembling sheriff.

" He is welcome," replied Will ; " if he pays honestly, I fancy there is a somewhat long score he has still to settle with me."

" Elevate him to a high position on yonder oak and save him from the gallows," suggested Much, who also had a score to settle on his own account.

" No," said Robin, " he came here on my invitation, and he shall have safe conduct back ; it is for him to choose whether he sups and pays, or pays without supping."

" Take what I have," cried the sheriff, " only let me begone " ; and he threw the bag of gold upon the ground.

" Wait a moment," said Robin, " I cannot appear

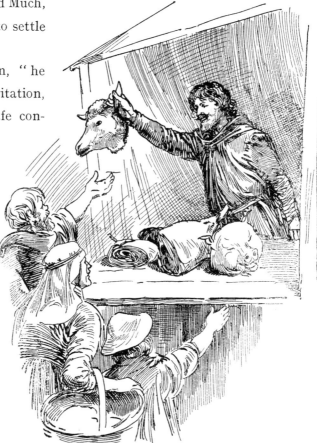

' Selling the same quantity of meat for a penny as the others gave for five "—(See p. 64).

before my wife like a common butcher, and methinks your doublet and cloak would suit me uncommonly well. By your leave we shall make an exchange."

In a trice the men had pulled their victim from his horse and stripping off his clothes arrayed him in the garments that Robin discarded. They placed him on the butcher's nag and brought him out of the wood, and as he rode sadly home he could hear the peals of laughter behind him. Trusting that the darkness would shield him from inquisitive eyes, he sneaked to his home ; but his cook, who bore him little goodwill, got hold of the tale of his misadventure, and next day all Nottingham was laughing at the joke.

Little John had been out hunting, and on his return his comrades related with great gusto the history of Robin's enterprise as a butcher and the consequences that followed his escapade.

" It was a merry prank," quoth Little John ; " methinks I must go to Nottingham one day, for I have never been there."

The others expressed surprise at this, and it transpired that he was a North Countryman, and since he came to the forest had never felt the inclination or curiosity to travel beyond its borders.

" Why not go to-morrow ? " suggested Robin, " there is to be an archery bout ; perhaps the sheriff will offer the butcher's nag as the first prize."

A roar of laughter greeted this sally, for the horse was knock-kneed and blind in one eye.

Little John followed Robin's advice and departed early next day for Nottingham. He was directed to the Square before the Castle, and joined the archers who were to shoot at and split a willow-wand, a performance that required much more skill than the customary practice of aiming at the butts. Little John was the only successful competitor in all three rounds of the trial ; he split the wand each time, whilst the others shot wide of the mark. The sheriff, who adjudged the prizes, applauded loudly.

"By my troth!" he cried, " I have never seen a better archer, and our men here are not lacking in skill ! Whence do you come, my fine fellow, and what is your name ? "

"The outlaw was the life and soul of the party"—(See p. 65).

Nothing abashed, Little John replied that he came from Holderness, and his name was Reynold Greenleaf. Now the sheriff had for some time been on the look out for a strong man to act as his bodyguard, for he went in wholesome terror of Robin Hood and his men, whenever he ventured beyond the city walls. Here was the very fellow he required ; it seemed to him quite providential that he had come across him.

"My good fellow," he said ingratiatingly, " would you not like to be my servant ? I would treat you well and pay you twenty marks a year, for, on my faith, an archer like you is not to be met with every

"Would you not like to be my servant?"—(See p. 69).

day—save perchance amongst those ruffians in Sherwood," he added, as a recollection of yesterday's indignities burst upon his mind.

Little John accepted the offer with alacrity. Here was an opportunity to see something of town life free of expense, and at the same time he resolved that he would be the worst servant that master ever had.

Once established in the sheriff's house, Little John found his duties light. He was expected to accompany his master whenever he went abroad on duty or pleasure, and to give exhibitions of his archery as an entertainment to guests.

All went smoothly for a time ; but one morning Little John overslept, and when he came down at noon found that the sheriff had gone out hunting with some of his friends without troubling about his bodyguard. He made his way to the buttery where the food and wine were kept, and demanded his dinner ; but the butler, who was jealous of the new servant, seized the opportunity to display his petty spite. He locked the door behind him and declared that he had no orders from his master, and could dispense neither meat nor drink without them.

" You must await the master's return," he affirmed, and put the key of the door in his pocket.

The hungry man was at the end of his patience, so he raised his foot and gave the butler a mighty kick which doubled the latter up, and he lay upon the floor as though he never meant to rise again.

It was the work of a moment for Little John to force open the door and enter the buttery, where he speedily made inroads upon pasties, cold game and plum pudding indiscriminately, for he was a doughty trencherman and his appetite had been sharpened by his long fast.

Meanwhile the butler lay in the passage and yelled for help, whereat the cook came to see what was the matter.

" Here's a pretty state of affairs, and company coming to supper," he exclaimed when he beheld the wreckage of his choice confections, and he dealt Little John three resounding blows on the back with the hilt of his short sword.

The big man turned round, his mouth full of cream tart.

" Why, cook," said he as soon as he could speak, " you have a brawny arm, and now that I have eaten my fill I would have a bout with you for exercise."

The cook was nothing loth, and advanced with his drawn sword, whilst the butler, who could still not straighten himself, crawled out of the way and went to his bed, where he lay moaning for the rest of the day.

Up and down the long passage Little John and the cook fought for an hour and more, but so evenly matched were they that neither could inflict a blow upon the other. At length tired out they threw down their swords and Little John held out his hand, saying, " Byrlady, you are too good a man to spend your life toasting your nose near the gridiron. Come with me to the greenwood and Robin Hood will give you

"It was the work of a moment . . . to force
open the door"—(See p. 71).

twenty marks a year, two suits of livery and a free and merry life, with choicest game and venison for the asking."

"That's the very place for me," agreed the cook with enthusiasm. "Let us drink a horn of wine in good fellowship and be off before the master comes home."

They plighted their friendship in a bottle of the sheriff's choicest sack, and feasted upon humble-pie and wheaten bread, the cook listening between whiles with open mouth to Little John's accounts of his exploits in the forest.

"I care not to go empty-handed like a beggar to Robin Hood," said the former, "whilst there are stores of silver plate here that we could take with us. It is really fine stuff, for most of it has been extorted, at different times, from the Saxon gentry hereabouts. The sheriff has a wonderfully taking way with him when he fancies anything!"

"I vow," acquiesced his companion, "it would be doing a kindness to your master to relieve him of some of his surplus store; it will save him the trouble of looking after it."

They finished their repast and hastened to the store-room, where they wrenched off the strong steel locks from chests and cupboards, and possessed themselves of silver vessels, plates and cups and over three hundred pounds in money.

Shouldering their bundles they stepped out briskly until they reached the trysting tree in the forest. A blast from Little John's horn soon assembled Robin and his band, all of whom were delighted to see their comrade return safe and sound after his long absence.

"God greet you, dear master," said Little John, "I am right glad to be at home again ; and as you see I come not alone, for the sheriff has sent you his cook, his silver plate and three hundred and three pounds in sterling gold."

"You are welcome," spoke Robin to the cook, "and I trust you will abide here with us, for you are as stalwart a man as ever I did see ; but I swear the sheriff never sent willingly these gifts to me."

"Think you I would deceive you, master," avowed Little John ; "nay, I can prove to the contrary by bringing the sheriff himself to see you."

He did not wait for leave, but ran off as hard as he could, five

"Little John and the cook fought for an hour or more"—(See p. 71).

miles and more, until he came to the favourite hunting place of the sheriff and his friends. Agreeably to his expectations the cry, " Tally ho, tally ho," met his ears, and his late master came riding along with the huntsman and hounds.

" Why, Reynold Greenleaf, where have you been all day ? " questioned the sheriff, pulling up. " I forgot all about you when we left this morning."

" I have been in the forest," was the reply, " and I saw a marvellous sight ; you would hardly credit it, for there stood a splendid hart with a herd of seven score deer behind him and all of them were green. I did not dare attack them ; the stag looked so savage I ran away."

" That must be a sight worth seeing," said the sheriff. " Think you you could find the spot again, perchance they might still be there ? "

Little John urged the sheriff to leave his friends and hasten, if he wished to reach the place whilst daylight lasted, and catching the stirrup leather he ran alongside the horse until they emerged from the brushwood. Immediately in front of them was a giant oak, and round about its great trunk stood seven score men in Lincoln-green with Robin Hood foremost amongst them.

" Woe betide you, Reynold Greenleaf ; you have betrayed me basely," said the sheriff, stopping horror-stricken at the sight.

" That's your own fault," retorted Little John, " for going out hunting and leaving me at home to starve. I promise you we shall not treat you so scurvily here."

He thereupon begged Robin to treat the sheriff to his best, so that he might learn a lesson in hospitality from the outlaws. The sheriff, having no other choice, sat down to table with the others ; but his appetite did not improve when he observed that the meal was served on his own silver plate and the wine in his finest embossed flagons.

" Be of good cheer," said Robin kindly, " for though you richly deserve hanging, your life will be spared, because Little John has asked this boon for you."

" It grows dark, you are sure to lose your way in the forest," broke in Friar Tuck cheerfully, " and that will be worse than the gallows, for the wood is haunted o'nights, and many a traveller have we found quite mazed in the morning."

The sheriff shivered, for he was superstitious and the way was long and lonely. There seemed nothing for it but to beg a night's shelter of the outlaws, which he did with a very bad grace.

A smile passed round the company when Robin politely regretted that he had no spare bed to offer his guest. " Indeed," said he, " thanks to you, we are denizens of the greenwood and frequently obliged to sleep out of doors, so you can make no ob_jection to do as we do."

Nevertheless the sheriff did make most vigorous objections, but to no avail; he was courteously con-

" They . . . possessed themselves of silver vessels "—(See p. 72).

ducted out of doors, and with a guard of hardy men, who thought nothing of a night spent in the open, he was obliged to lie on the cold, damp ground, with the wind nipping his very bones.

In the early morning, before any one else was stirring, Marian brought him a horn of hot sack, and never before had any beverage seemed so delicious ; it warmed his aching body and enabled him to get up and prepare for his homeward journey.

Robin came out cheerful and smiling.

" Do you not find life in the greenwood very jolly, master sheriff ? " he inquired. " Where can one repose more sweetly than on the lap of Mother Earth ? "

" It is harder than the floor of a penitent's cell," replied the sheriff, " and I would rather lie in my grave than spend another night under such conditions."

" You surprise me," said Robin mendaciously. " I thought of keeping you here for at least a year so that you might learn the charms of an outlaw's life."

The sheriff, thoroughly alarmed at Robin's words, pleaded to be allowed to go home at once.

" Out of your charity, intercede for me, dear lady," he begged, turning to Marian. " I shall be the best friend the outlaws ever had if I go safely hence."

Marian's kind heart was touched by this plea, and she added her entreaties to his.

" I can deny you nothing, dear wife," said Robin, and drawing out his sword he ordered the sheriff to promise on his honour not to molest the merrie men or their leaders in the future.

The sheriff swore a mighty oath that by sea nor land, by day nor night they would suffer neither harm nor hindrance from him

or by his
orders.

With this
promise on his
lips, and a
determination
to break it at
the first op-
portunity in
his heart, the
sheriff rode
away, vowing
he would
never again
enter the
greenwood as
long as he
lived.

"Seven score men in Lincoln-green"—(See p. 74).

CHAPTER VIII

"Robin Hood and Little John,
    They are both gone to fair O ;
And we will go to the merry green-wood,
    To see what they do there O."

DURING the remainder of the winter the sheriff brooded over the
indignities to which he had been subjected by Robin Hood, and at
length, after much cogitation, devised a means whereby he hoped to get
his enemy into his power. In pursuance of this idea he made a proclamation that this year the May-day revels would be rendered especially
attractive by an archery tournament, in which all the best bowmen of

the North were invited to take part. As first prize he offered a magnificent golden-headed arrow with a silver shaft a yard long. He also let it be known that fair treatment and safe-conduct would be meted out to all comers, reckoning that this tempting bait would lure Robin and his companions into the city, and once there, he made a vow they should not again escape him. He arranged to have a force of armed men in readiness, and upon a signal from him they were to arrest every man in Lincoln-green they could lay their hands upon.

The tidings reached Robin as he stood in the greenwood, in his favourite attitude, with his back against a tree, enjoying the sweet springtide and the scent of its thousand blossoms. In a moment the charms of nature were forgotten and with a blast of his horn he summoned his company to share the news with them.

"Hurrah!" he cried, "we shall show them who are the best shots in the North Country, or in all merry England for that matter;" but Marian, ever wise in counsel, shook her head doubtfully.

"Do not go, dear Robin," she advised. "I feel sure the sheriff contemplates some treachery towards you; not for one moment would I trust his word of honour."

"I think you are right," agreed Little John; "it will not do to try his good faith too far."

"Maybe, maybe," said Robin testily, "but I mean to go and see the fun, and those of you who are not cowards will come with me, I doubt not."

The word "coward" stuck in the men's throat, and now not one of them would have remained at home for all the gold in England. Friar Tuck and Maid Marian alone declined to take part in such a harebrained adventure.

In order to run as little risk as possible it was decided that the

Lincoln-green must be discarded for the nonce, in favour of country-men's suits, so that they could mingle undetected amongst the populace. Robin arranged that Little John, Will Scarlet, Much, and one " Gilbert with the White Hand," all famous marksmen, were to shoot with him, whilst the others should keep watch, with bows ready bent in case of treachery.

On the eventful day the Castle Square presented an animated appear-ance ; lads and lasses danced about the garlanded maypole in the centre, and in various parts games and trials of strength or skill were in progress. In one corner a crowd assembled round some country yokels, who had a " grinning match," whilst the diminutive pig, that was to be awarded

for the broadest grin, ran squealing amongst the feet of the specta-tors. In another part a palmer newly re-turned from the Holy Land sold sacred relics ; but the centre of at-traction for the ma-jority of the holiday makers was the archery butts, where some fine shooting was to be seen. Time after time the arrows struck so close to the centre of the target that the on-lookers cheered lustily.

" With a blast of his horn he summoned his company "—(See p. 78).

Some cried, " Blue wins," others " 'Tis yellow," or " Brown has got it," as each of Robin's picked men took their aim ; but a man in red stepped forward and hit the bull's-eye three times in succession with such apparent ease that the observers held their breath in amazement. As a final test of skill a willow wand was placed before the butts, and the excitement of the crowd knew no bounds when the man in red split it straight through the centre at a distance of 150 yards, a feat that had seldom been surpassed.

The sheriff gazed mistrustfully at the man in red as he handed him the much-desired prize, but Robin was cleverly disguised, and he was not sure, until something familiar in the gait and a turn of the head changed his suspicions into certainty. He gave his prearranged signal to his foresters, who made a dash towards the group of which Robin was the centre ; but the outlaws were too quick for them, and surrounded their master with arrows quivering on their strings ready for flight.

Then ensued a scene of unparalleled uproar and confusion, swords clashing, arrows flying, women shrieking, children trampled under foot, the crowd pressing here, retreating there, leaving a trail of wounded and crushed in its path.

Little John received a severe wound in the knee and, faint from loss of blood, sank to the ground in the midst of the mêlée.

" I pray you, master," said he, " take your sword and slay me, for I can go no further and never will I be taken alive ; kill me so that I do not hinder your progress."

" Not for all the gold in England would I desert you, my friend," replied Robin ; " we must make a stand and defend you to the last."

" God forbid such a folly," cried Much, raising the giant by an almost superhuman effort to his shoulder and, placing him upon his back,

"THE KING! THE KING!"
(See Ch. 10).

carried his burden bravely, stopping ever and anon to shoot and then going on again.

"To the gates," shouted the outlaws, "our men hold them for us," and after a desperate struggle they managed to pass unscathed beyond the walls.

They were now free of the mob, so turning round they poured a volley into the midst of the sheriff's men, who were pursuing them. Not a single dart was wasted, every arrow met its mark, and those who escaped the onslaught broke and fled in all directions. This gave Robin and his men time to reach the friendly shelter of the woods, and Much was relieved of Little John's weight. A rude litter was constructed and the wounded man placed upon it ; but his condition was so serious that it was decided to cut across by Barnsdale to Lea Castle, the seat of Sir Richard, which was only a short distance away.

The Castle, an imposing edifice strongly fortified and surrounded by a double moat, was soon reached, and Sir Richard welcomed his friends with hospitable delight. Little John was at once placed under Lady Richard's motherly care, for she—like most good housewives in those days—was well versed in the virtues of herb medicines and the tending of wounds. Satisfied that his faithful comrade was in good hands, Robin thanked Sir Richard and prepared to take his leave ; but he had reckoned without his host, for that kindly gentleman flatly refused to permit one of his visitors to depart. Robin expostulated, pointing out that in addition to the expense of entertaining over seven score hungry men, the knight ran a grave risk in harbouring outlaws who were flying from the enraged authorities at Nottingham. Sir Richard listened politely to Robin's remarks ; but refused to be convinced of anything save that his friends were in his house, and that they should not depart without accepting his hospitality. He dispatched a messenger to bring

F

"Lads and lasses danced about the garlanded maypole"—(See p. 79).

back Maid Marian and Friar Tuck, and thus complete the merry party that met around his board that night.

Meanwhile there was a hue and cry after the fugitives, who were finally tracked to Lea Castle and the sheriff notified of the fact. He came helter-skelter to the Castle with four score men behind him, but found the gates closed, the drawbridge up and the walls manned by stout retainers. "Give up the enemies of the King," shouted the sheriff.

The knight mounted the wall and hurled back defiance.

"If you want them come in and fetch them yourself," he replied; and the sheriff realised that it was useless to bandy words or endeavour to make his way in with the small force at his disposal, so again helter-skelter back he went to Nottingham.

Next day he set out post haste for London to seek audience of the King. Richard, newly returned from the Crusades, listened sympathetically to his woes, for the sheriff was clever enough to gloss over his own shortcomings and paint the misdemeanours of his enemies in the darkest colours.

The King advised him to go home and get together all the good bow-men in the countryside and make Sir Richard of the Lea and Robin Hood prisoners wherever and whenever he could. The sheriff looked dubious.

" 'Tis easier said than done, sire," said he.

" If you do not succeed," promised Richard, " I shall come within a month and rout out the redoubtable Robin and all his gang myself."

As there remained nothing else to do, the sheriff collected a strong force and marched to Sherwood ; but the outlaws were as elusive as a will-o'-the-wisp. After several vain attempts to find them, he marched his men back again to Nottingham, amidst the jeers of the mob, whose sympathies were with Robin Hood, the protector of the poor. The sheriff determining not to be baulked of his vengeance, set to work to entrap that gentle knight, Sir Richard of the Lea, who all unsuspecting of the designs against him, went out one morn with his hawk upon his wrist. He loosed the bird by the riverside, and as he stood there, alone and unprotected, he was suddenly surrounded by a hostile band who made him prisoner and led him away. Lady Richard, watching from the Castle tower, was witness of her lord's betrayal without being able to deliver him, their retainers being too few in number to attack so large a force. Without losing a moment she mounted her palfrey and rode to the greenwood to seek aid of Robin Hood. She had scarce uttered her story before Robin and all his men were off hot-foot, stopping neither for hedge nor ditch, away, away, on a mad chase towards Nottingham. They were just in time to conceal themselves, as only the merrie men knew how, amongst the trees and scrub that formed a belt outside the city walls, when the procession hove into sight with the sheriff riding in front and, walking beside his horse, Sir Richard, in shackles.

" Bide your time, my men," said Robin, " there is a mark for each one ; see that you miss it not ; but leave the sheriff to me."

All at once like a " bolt from the blue " a flight of arrows darted in amongst the marching men, and the procession came to a disorderly halt. A second shower of arrows did deadly work and many men fell on the roadside never to rise again.   Those who escaped were in too great a haste to seek the shelter of the city to trouble about the prisoner or stay to investigate the cause of their rout.

The outlaws rushed from their ambush and loosing Sir Richard's bonds guided him rapidly into the forest before pursuit became possible.   With feelings of true joy and thankfulness they handed him over to the embraces of his wife and the tender care of Maid Marian, and it was decided that for the present they would remain at the Lodge in the forest, in case of further molestation from the authorities.

The sheriff meanwhile lay stark and stiff in a ditch by the roadside, pierced in the back by the silver arrow with a golden head that he himself had placed in Robin Hood's hand.

They carried him home feet foremost, and there was not one in all that city who regretted his death, or remembered a single deed of kindness or charity on his part.

On the day following the rescue of Sir Richard, Marian begged Robin to go fishing in a stream, some distance off, famed for its fine trout.

" We must give the old folks more delicate fare than we require," said the thoughtful hostess.   " They are still somewhat upset after their unpleasant adventure."

Robin, only too happy to please his kind wife, set out early and had a good day's sport.

As he was on the homeward way, he came unexpectedly upon the Bishop of Hereford travelling with a large number of retainers.

There was no time to summon aid, and with the events of Allen-a-Dale's and his own wedding fresh in his memory, the outlaw concluded

that his only means of safety lay in flight.   He took to his heels and ran
to a small cottage that his sharp eye had espied in a hollow near by.
The door stood open revealing an old woman within, bending over her
distaff.

" Good dame," he panted, " save me, I am pursued and sore pressed."

" Why, who are you ? " inquired the old woman.

" Robin Hood, the outlaw, and the Bishop of Hereford with his men
are close behind ; if they catch me they will bring me to the gallows for
sure."

" Aye ! " said the dame.   " I know you now, good Robin, you brought
me some hose and shoes one Saturday night not so long ago.   We poor
folk have too few friends
to forget any of them.
Now tell me where I can
best hide you ? "

Robin looked round
the humble cottage, and
could see no possible
place of concealment, so
he begged the good
woman to change clothes
with him, which she did
without   the   slightest
demur.   The transforma-
tion was quickly effected,
and Robin clad in robe,
shawl and cap, whilst the
old wife cut a sorry figure
in doublet and hose of

" His only means of safety lay in flight "—(See p. 85).

"'Good dame,' he panted, 'save me'"—(See p. 85).

Lincoln-green. After assuring her that she need have no fear for her safety, he hobbled out of the cottage and passed the bishop and his retainers, who were too busy searching amongst the bushes, for the outlaw, to trouble themselves a b o u t the beldame going by with her spindle in her hand. He soon reached the greenwood, where at first his comrades did not recognize him in his novel attire, and prepared for the rescue of the old woman should she be in jeopardy on his account.

The search amongst the bushes proving fruitless, one of the retainers suggested looking inside the cottage; and the bishop turned hopefully in that direction. At first glance the place seemed empty; but further search revealed a figure huddled up in a dark corner.

"We have him," cried the retainer triumphantly. "And a rare ugly one he is too," added another. "Guard him well," the bishop ordered, as he mounted his horse, "and see that he does not escape you."

He rode along chuckling and congratulating himself on his easy catch, until a sudden turn of the narrow path brought him headlong into the serried ranks of Robin's company drawn across the road, headed by their leader, Little John and Will Scarlet who stood with drawn swords close to the nose of the bishop's horse.

" Who dares to bar my progress on the King's highway ? " demanded the bishop.

" Robin Hood ! " was the curt reply, as he caught the bridle in his free hand.

" That cannot be," said a weak, quavery voice, " Robin Hood is my prisoner and walks bound behind me."

" I would fain see your prisoner," said Robin. " Let him be brought here."

At this the old dame hobbled forward and honoured the bishop with a profound curtsy, and a roar of laughter broke from the men when they beheld the supposed Robin Hood.

" Fie, Sir Bishop," admonished Robin. " I blush to think that you should try to run away with a charming and virtuous lady, and then show her such scant courtesy as to permit her to go afoot whilst you are riding."

" Off from the horse," cried a dozen voices, and willing hands dragged the prelate from his saddle and hoisted the old lady in his place.

" Pay your toll and go your way," said Robin, examining the contents of the saddle bags. The search was rewarded by the find of £500, which he divided into two parts, one for his men and the remainder for the old dame, who was thus enabled to live in comfort the rest of her days.

" Now let him go," ordered Robin, " I have no desire for his company."

"Not yet," clamoured Friar Tuck, "let him sing us a Mass first, I fain would hear his sweet voice again."

The bishop protested, but to no avail, for they bound him fast to a tree and threatened to leave him there until he complied. He mumbled through the sacred service most unwillingly, despite the reverent attention of all the company, who were God-fearing men although they led such rough lives. In those days when every man had to protect himself, and there was little justice meted out to those who had no influence, the taking of life, and robbery, were not considered the serious offences they are to-day. Nor must it be forgotten that Robin Hood and his company never interfered with the good and worthy members of the Church, of which there were many even in those times; but they waged war on those wicked priests who robbed and oppressed the poor.

When he had performed his duty, the bishop was unbound and placed at liberty; whereupon his temper getting the better of his discretion, he roundly cursed Robin Hood and his

"They mounted the bishop backwards on his horse"—(See p. 89).

associates, and wound up with a particularly malevolent one in Latin for the poor old dame, who smiled and thanked him under the impression that he had pronounced a blessing.

The men were so enraged at this behaviour that as a punishment they mounted the bishop backwards on his horse, and putting the tail in his hand forced him to ride through the forest in this undignified position, exhorting him meanwhile to reverse his curse and pray for Robin Hood.

CHAPTER IX

"I dwell by dale and downe, quoth hee,
   And Robin to take· Ime sworne;
 And when I am called by my right name
   I am Guy of good Gisborne."

Robin Hood and Guy of Gisborne.

THE King was as good as his word and came to Nottingham as he had promised. The newly - appointed sheriff was very zealous in apprising His Grace of Robin's misdeeds and furnished his own version of the events that led to the death of his predecessor. Lion Heart listened unmoved to this recital; the loss of an easily-replaced sheriff and a few of his men did not greatly affect him, and the bold audacity of the outlaw appealed to his own courageous nature. He was inclined to regard Robin's shortcomings with leniency, until one day he went hunting in Sherwood Forest, and discovered how his herds of deer had been thinned by the depredations of the "merrie men." He was quick to resent this interference with his favourite pastime, and it hardened his determination to get hold of the whole band and subject the leaders to condign punishment. So Lion Heart made his plans; but they went astray, and his intended vengeance remained an empty threat, for Robin and his men had disappeared, none knew whither.

When news was brought that Richard had come with a large force
of soldiers to Nottingham, Robin decided to disband his company for a
short time. He was too loyal to rebel against his sovereign, and for once
held it no disgrace to run away instead of fighting.

Sir Guy Gamwell and his lady were living in retirement at a small
place on the coast (now known as Robin Hood's Bay), and Will, being
desirous of visiting his parents, persuaded Robin and Marian to accompany him thither. Friar Tuck, Little John and Much remained in the
forest, declaring that it was the only place in which to live. Sir Richard
of the Lea and his wife were safely placed with friends in a remote part
of the country, and the men dispersed to various places in the vicinity
of their old haunts. The Allen-a-Dales, who had now two sturdy sons,
lived in the old home in the Dale where Allen was born ; but they always
declared that their happiest days were those they had spent in the
greenwood.

It was a pleasant meeting between the Gamwells and their old friends,
and Sir Guy could scarce credit that the great bearded man was his son
Will, until the latter convinced him by doffing his cap and displaying
his unmistakable red poll.

Robin and Marian, wandering along the shore happy as children on a
holiday, were untiring in their efforts to aid the poor fisherfolk, who were
suffering hard times owing to the depredations of French vessels that
were continually raiding the coast. Whilst occupied in these deeds of
kindness the time sped quickly, until one day Robin was summoned back
to Sherwood by a message that caused him the liveliest misgivings. Friar
Tuck reported that Little John had ventured into Nottingham some days
previously and, not having returned, grave fears were entertained for
his safety. The outlaw decided to return at once, and, leaving Will to
follow at leisure with Maid Marian, rode off at a gallop.

He reached Barnsdale without adventure and was about to enter a well-known path when he was accosted by a knight clad in heavy armour.

"Good-morrow, my fine fellow," said the knight. "I am doubtful of the way, this wood is unfamiliar to me."

Robin inquired whither he desired to go, and offered to guide him, for which courtesy the knight thanked him, and said he was seeking an outlaw called Robin Hood, whose head he intended carrying to the King.

Robin dismounted and, tying his horse to a tree, replied—

"Come with me, my brave friend, you shall have the pleasure of beholding him whom you seek; but before we go let us have a little sport under the greenwood trees; for judging by the bow you carry, you should be a good archer."

The knight complied and helped to cut a briar, which they set up as a target. The first time Robin shot, he missed by an inch, his opponent by a foot. The second time the knight missed again; but Robin displayed his marksmanship by cleaving the slender briar in two.

"Well done," cried the stranger, "I doubt if the renowned Robin Hood himself can better that. Pray tell me your name, for I am proud to know a man of your skill."

"Nay," answered the outlaw, "that will I not, until I am acquainted with yours."

The other drew himself up proudly, saying, "I am Guy of Gisborne, and have sworn, on my knightly honour, not to return to Nottingham until I have slain the outlaw Robin Hood."

"My life is yours, if you can take it," answered Robin, doffing his cap, "for I am he you seek."

The knight started at this intelligence, and, without further parley both drew their swords to attack one another in no friendly spirit. They fought long together, thrusting and parrying, a well-matched pair; but

Robin, having caught his foot in the root of a tree, stumbled and almost fell. Before he could recover himself, Sir Guy seized this advantage, and dealt him such a blow in the ribs that Robin sank to the ground half-stunned. The knight approached his foe and would have despatched him, there and then, had Robin not sprung up suddenly, and with a single cut sent Sir Guy reeling lifeless against a tree. Struck by an idea, Robin pulled off his clothes, clad himself in the garments and armour of the dead knight, and took possession of an uncommon little silver bugle that was strung round his neck. Feeling secure in this disguise he turned in the direction of Nottingham, and ventured into the city with a view of finding out what had befallen his faithful friend.

He had only ridden a short distance when his progress was interrupted by a throng of people, who stood gazing expectantly towards the Castle. Upon questioning a yeoman on the edge of the crowd, he learnt that they were waiting to see a noted outlaw, known as Little John, go forth to be hanged on a tree at the edge of the wood, as a warning to similar male-factors. Owing to previous experience the sheriff had given orders that no one was to be permitted to approach the place of execution, save the officials connected with the hanging, so as to prevent any attempt at a rescue, " though there is little chance of that," added his informant, " since they say Robin Hood has left this part of the country for good."

Robin did not wait to hear any more; but returned to the wood and concealed himself behind a clump of trees some little distance from the oak that had been prepared as a gallows for the outlaw. As soon as he saw the sheriff and his cortege approaching with the prisoner, Robin rode towards them, blowing cheerily on the silver bugle.

" Hark ! " said the sheriff. " I hear Sir Guy of Gisborne's bugle sounding in the wood. Look ! there he comes ; I can see his armour glittering in the sunshine."

Robin rode up to the group standing by the oak tree, and Little John could scarce repress a cry of joy, for he recognized his master at once. Fortunately the sheriff, who was short-sighted, accepted the newcomer as Sir Guy of Gisborne, without question, and the hangman and his attendants, being occupied with their business, did not trouble their heads about the matter at all.

" Good morrow, my fine fellow "—
(See p. 91).

" Welcome, Sir Guy," said the sheriff, advancing to meet him, " your merry note tells me that you have successfully accomplished your mission, and we are at length rid of that pest, Robin Hood."

" The body lies in the wood, you need but to send and fetch it," replied Robin, smiling grimly.

" You have well-earned your fee, Sir Guy, and it shall be paid, as arranged, in sterling gold," quoth the sheriff.

" Pray do not mention the matter," returned the other politely. " I do not want the money, the service I have rendered is its own reward ; but if you are willing to grant a favour, I would ask you to permit me to slay yon servant, in the same manner that I requited his master."

" By all means," said the sheriff, delighted to get off so cheaply ; " since you are so easily satisfied, I would not gainsay you."

Robin thereupon approached Little John with sword upraised as though to slay him.

"Confess your sins, for you are about to die," he cried; then turning to the sheriff and his men he begged them to stand back a little, as it was contrary to all custom for so many to listen to the shrift.

Somewhat abashed by this rebuke they did his bidding, and Robin was left alone with the prisoner. He pulled his horse up close beside

"Robin . . . sent Sir Guy reeling lifeless against a tree" — (See p. 92).

the latter and, bending down as though to hear better, quickly cut the bonds and whispered, "Jump behind me." Without a moment's hesitation, Little John leapt behind his master, who dug his spurs into his mettlesome horse and galloped away, before the onlookers realized what had occurred.

As soon as it was safe to slacken speed, Robin requested Little John to relate how he came to be in such a dilemma as that from which he had just escaped. The latter, looking very shamefaced, confessed that he had found time hang heavily in the greenwood, without his comrades, so he donned the dress of a beggar and went to Nottingham in search of amusement. He entered an inn where the company was convivial; but presently a dispute arose, and the argument becoming heated, a fight ensued in which Little John took an active part. The affray terminated in his being dragged, in company with his companions, before the sheriff, where he was recognized by the butler, who at once denounced him, as a return favour for the kick that he had not yet forgotten.

"That is the story," said he, "and but for you, dear master, it would have finished its last chapter on the branch of an oak at the edge of the wood, with never a priest to say Amen!"

"Little John," said Robin a few days later, when the company were all assembled again, "the treasury is empty, do you go out begging and see how fortune favours you."

"I am ready, master," quoth the other, "but I think a palmer's dress will be most suitable and becoming for the occasion, with a staff for my comfort, and a bag for my spoil."

The idea being approved, Little John donned a palmer's habit, and went along the highway. Presently he encountered four beggars;

"What is your direction?"—
(See p. 96).

one was deaf and dumb, another blind, and two limped behind on crutches.

"Good-morrow, brothers," said Little John. "What is your direction? I fain would travel in your company."

"We like not your ugly face," answered the blind man; "nor your manner of speech," added the deaf and dumb one; "so clear out or we shall make it hot for you," exclaimed one cripple as he landed a lusty kick on the palmer's person.

"Is that how you feel?" said the latter, rolling up his sleeves. "Well, I am willing to oblige all four of you, so come along and fight it out, singly or together as you please." Little John wasted no time in parley, he nipped the dumb man till he roared for mercy, he made the blind one "see stars," and he who had been a cripple for seven years and more, ran away with a celerity that proved his cure complete.

Taking the remaining three together, Little John banged them against a wall, and his heart beat high with hope when he heard the ring of money in the bags they carried.

"Little John banged them against a wall"—(See p. 96).

In a trice he grabbed the bags and was out of sight ere the beggars could recover themselves, and they, finding pursuit useless, went grumbling on their way. Little John returned to the trysting tree, clinking twenty pounds in gold and silver, and feeling very much pleased at the result of this little essay as a beggar.

CHAPTER X

" Hear undernead dis laith stean
laiz robert earl of Huntingtun
near arcir ver az hie sa geud
an pipl kauld im robin heud
sick utlawz as hi an iz men
vil england nivr si agen.
    obiit 24. kal. dekembris 1247."
        Epitaph on Robin Hood.

FOR six months King Richard waited at Nottingham ; but never once did he catch a glimpse of Robin nor his men, for they had disappeared as completely as though the earth had opened and swallowed them up. The capture and rescue of Little John added fresh fuel to Lion Heart's desire to come face to face with the daring outlaw ; so he eagerly fell in with the suggestion made by one of his foresters, to be led by him to some of Robin's favourite haunts, with which he professed to be familiar.

" Take five trusty knights with you," counselled the man, " disguise yourselves as monks, and with me to guide you, I'll warrant to show you Robin Hood if he be still in the neighbourhood."

They sent to a neighbouring monastery to borrow cowls and gowns, and habited in these the party set out, under the guidance of the forester, King Richard, garbed like an abbot, riding in front. They had penetrated about a mile down a long glade of lime-trees when they were confronted by Robin and some of his men. The former seized the bridle of the King's horse and said civilly—

" Sir Abbot, I would have a word with you, by your leave. We are dwellers of this forest, living upon the King's deer, other expedients have we none, so we pray you give us out of your plenty in the name of charity."

" I am on my way back from Nottingham where I have spent two weeks with the King. If you are in any way acquainted with the customs of a royal Court, you will understand why forty pounds is all that remains to me of the large sum of money I took with me. To that amount you are welcome," replied the King as he handed over his purse.

Robin waved back the proffered gift.

" Keep it," said he, " we only take from those who have more than their needs, and I trow the Court leeches have already sucked you dry enough, we shall not add robbery to your misfortunes. Since you have so lately seen our King," he continued, " I prithee stay awhile as my honoured guest and over a stoup of wine give us tidings of our brave Cœur de Lion, whom we all love."

The supposed abbot signified his willingness to share the cheer of his new-found friends, whereat Robin blew a blast upon his horn. From all directions came stalwart bowmen, swift as the deer they loved to chase, and, forming in rows in front of their master, fell upon one knee with a military precision, that greatly impressed the warrior monarch. At a signal, the archers formed into a guard of honour and escorted the guest and his followers to the Lodge, where a meal was quickly prepared and served with the open-handed hospitality that distinguished the outlaws.

The King, attended on assiduously by Robin and Little John, and seated beside Maid Marian whose beauty and wit could be surpassed by none of the Court ladies, enjoyed the impromptu repast to the full.

He laughed loudly at Friar Tuck's jokes, listened with interest to the outlaw's tales of derring-doe, and noted how loyal they were to King and Country. He learnt much about the evils and oppression his Saxon subjects suffered, and made a silent vow to do his best to right the wrong.

When the meal was finished they repaired to the greenwood at Richard's request, as he was desirous of witnessing a display of archery from those bowmen whose fame had spread all over England.

Two slender wands were set up for targets within a garland of woodland blossoms, and the condition was made that any marksman whose arrow fell outside the wreath, or injured a single flowér, should forfeit his arrows to Robin and receive a buffet on the head in exchange. Although Richard maintained that the distance between the archers and the target was a full fifty paces too long, few failed to hit within the garland ; but those who were unsuccessful submitted to their punishment good-temperedly and joined in the laughter at their expense. Robin split the wand twice, with his wonted skill ; but the third time he failed the mark, and his dart fell a finger length outside the garland.

" A bad miss for you, master, you have lost your arrows and must pay the forfeit," shouted the men gleefully, for they thought it would be rare fun to see the hitter hit.

" What's sauce for the goose is sauce for the gander," said Robin, " so Sir Abbot, I deliver up my arrows to you, and I pray you give me my pay." The King hesitated, declaring that for one of his calling it was not seemly to smite so worthy a yeoman and perchance give him pain ; but Robin laughingly requested him to make no ceremony and hit his hardest.

" On your head be it," said Richard, rolling up his sleeve and delivering such a buffet that it felled the outlaw to the ground.

" In faith, there is pith in your arm, Sir Abbot," exclaimed Robin, and as he picked himself up he regarded his aggressor curiously, for in the act of raising his arm to strike, the abbot's hood had fallen back and revealed his features clearly.

The men were suddenly startled by their leader's cry, " The King !

the King! God save the King," and Robin fell to his knee pleading for mercy and pardon for himself and all his company. "We are rough fellows," said he, "but our hearts are true to you and 'Merry England.'"

"Get up, Robin," commanded the King, "I vow your knee is over-stiff in bending, for want of use. Your petition is granted upon the asking, but I attach a condition thereto."

"Sire, it is for you to command and for us to obey," replied Robin, whose voice could scarce be heard for the echoing of the men's cheers as they waved their caps and cried, "God save the King."

"And now for my condition, which is somewhat more of a desire; I would have you all return with me to London and remain there as my bodyguard," said Richard as he smilingly acknowledged the men's hearty salutation.

Robin's heart fell at these words, for they all loved the freedom and beauty of the forest, and he guessed the irksomeness of life at Court; but, there being no alternative, he concealed his chagrin and gratefully accepted the King's well-intentioned offer.

Marian, who had been a surprised spectator at these happenings, perceiving the monarch's kindly mood, now seized the favourable opportunity to plead the cause of those outraged knights, Sir Guy Gamwell and Sir Richard of the Lea.

"Who can refuse aught to so sweet a supplicant?" replied Richard graciously, and bidding the lady rise, he called to his knights to draw up a charter conferring upon both gentlemen the properties that had been filched from them; for the sheriff had seized Lea Castle in the name of the King, when Sir Richard was too far away to defend his home. The charters were duly signed and sealed and handed to Will Scarlet, who was to be the bearer of the good news to the two worthy noblemen and their patient wives.

The preparations for the departure were hastily accomplished, and the King and his knights clad in suits of Lincoln-green rode out of the forest with their escort of seven score " merrie men," and Robin, Marian and Little John were at the right and left hand of the valorous Lion Heart. Friar Tuck alone remained behind, declaring that life at Court had as little attraction for him as life in a convent, and he preferred to remain free in the greenwood so long as by strength, skill or cunning he could keep a well-stocked larder.

Dusk was falling as the jovial party passed through the city gates, and a pretty fright the townsfolk had, when the army in Lincoln-green clattered t h r o u g h the streets, singing and shouting all the way.

" The King has been slain," said they one to another, " and Robin Hood has come to take the city."

They scattered, like autumn leaves driven by the wind, before the invaders, and the King laughed long and loud as he observed the worthy citizens scuttling into their houses and making the

" Sir Abbot, I would have a word with you "—(See p. 97).

"The King . . . en-
joyed the impromptu
repast"—(See p. 98).

doors fast behind them.   Soon the streets were deserted by all save the
poorer inhabitants, who remained to cheer bold Robin Hood, for they
thought their deliverer had come at last.

When it was discovered that the King was riding in comradeship with
the outlaws the excitement knew no bounds, and there were many glum
faces in Nottingham Castle that day.

The sheriff was so overcome that he retired to his bed, and remained
there until the King and his train were well on their way to London.

Robin, faithful to his monarch's desire, remained at the Court and
was ever in high favour with the King; but the joy of life had gone for him
and he became melancholy, spending much time looking out of the
window at a group of trees in the palace grounds.   He scarce noted how,
day by day, his men deserted, until at length only his wife, Little John

and Will Scarlet remained to comfort and solace him. Marian pined like a caged bird, she missed her seven score merry children whom she had mothered and tended, and who loved her as she loved them, and tears fell from her eyes whenever she thought of the long, green glades of Sherwood.

At length Marian's failing health became so palpable that Richard was obliged to accede to Robin's oft-repeated petition and grant him leave to return to the greenwood.

" It shall be as you wish," said Richard, " but work no more mischief against my officers and let no man lose his life through your fault."

Robin readily promised that, so long as Richard lived, he would never raise his hand against any man, except in self-defence ; but he spoke no word in reply, when the monarch laughingly added, " And what about my deer, will you spare them too ? "

Joyfully the little band set their faces homeward, and when at length they caught a glimpse of the waving trees of Sherwood, they knelt down and offered up their thankfulness in prayer. They wandered down the well-known ways, where birds warbled a tuneful greeting and flowers wafted a perfumed message of welcome. Out of sheer joyousness Robin drew out his bugle and blew a blast that awakened the woodland echoes.

A moment later there was a stir and rustle, and through the brake and over the stream the " merrie men " came running and leaping as of yore. Robin and his companions could not stir, so great was their surprise, for they thought the company to be disbanded and dispersed.

" Welcome home ! " cried the men. " We are here awaiting you, dear master ; we knew you would come back at ast."

The old life was resumed and the band had many merry adventures and narrow escapes to its credit ; but the poor and the lowly always benefited by these escapades, and in many a humble cot the name of Robin Hood was never uttered without a blessing.

Ill-used nobles and yeomen fled to Sherwood in the troubled times of King John's reign, and Robin Hood assisted to gather together the army that gained for us the Great Charter signed at Runnymede, which was the beginning of freedom for the English people.

As the years passed away many of the "merrie men" passed with them. Will Scarlet was killed in the rebellion against John, and Much, the miller's son, fell at his side. Friar Tuck lived to a ripe old age, strong and jovial to the last, and was greatly missed by all those whom he had buffeted and ministered to, as occasion demanded.

Maid Marian did not long survive her home-coming to Sherwood, the trials of the sad year in London having undermined her health. When she had been tenderly laid to rest in the greenwood she so dearly loved, Robin made no outward manifestations of his grief, and his faithful friend Little John alone knew the pain in his master's lonely heart. Robin's hair grew grey and the strong back was no longer so upright, but he still led his men with all his old vigour.

When he was close upon eighty-six years old, he felt his strength waning and the quarter-staff became too heavy for his hands. "I am not well," said he to Little John, "methinks I may get relief at Kirklees Abbey, where my cousin, the abbess, has much renown for her skill in surgery."

"A happy thought," replied Little John hopefully, "we shall journey there without delay."

The abbess received her kinsman kindly and blooded the vein in his arm, a treatment that in those times was considered a cure for most ills ; but in her heart the treacherous woman bore the old man a grudge for some fancied slight in days of yore. Instead of binding his arm firmly she left the vein to bleed, so that Robin grew weaker hour by hour.

He had been placed on a bed in the abbess' private apartment, and Little John was abruptly dismissed and bidden not to return until the morrow.

As Robin felt his end approach, he raised his horn to his lips and blew a feeble blast. By good fortune Little John, seated in a copse near by, awaiting news of his master, heard the call and, suspecting something amiss, rushed to the convent door. It was fast locked and none answered his knocks, although they were loud enough to waken the dead. He put forth his great strength and, forcing the lock, made his way into the building. Not a soul was in sight as he hastened to the chamber where Robin lay; the door yielded easily and in a moment he was on his knee beside the bed. When he realized that his beloved master had been betrayed, his wrath was terrible to witness.

"I will burn Kirklees Abbey and all the nuns inside," he vowed passionately.

"Nay," whispered the dying man, "with my last breath I forbid it. In all my life I have never harmed a woman and will not do so at the end."

As the sun was setting he asked Little John to give him his bow. "I would fain shoot once more," he said.

His faithful friend lifted him up and carried him to the casement, placing the bent bow ready in his hand. With surprising strength Robin let the arrow fly, and it fell some distance off into the road beneath a group of trees.

"A blast that awakened the woodland echoes"—
(See p. 103).

" It is my last shot," he sighed. " Lay me where the arrow fell and put my bow beside me." Presently he said softly, " Little John, I hear Maid Marian calling," and with a happy smile he passed away in the arms of his true and faithful friend.

They buried him beneath the yews on the site marked by the arrow, and John Little blew the last blast on his master's bugle ere he laid it in the grave.

It was on the 18th day of November, 1247, in the reign of King Henry III that Robin breathed his last ; but he is not forgotten, nor will he be, so long as his spirit lives in the hearts of his countrymen.

" Robin let the arrow 'fly ". .(See p. 105).

The heritage he has left us manifests itself to-day when Englishmen rise in their millions to defend the weak and oppressed of other lands, crushed beneath the heel of a cruel and ruthless invader. It will be ours whilst we continue to cry in love and loyalty, as did Robin Hood nigh seven hundred years ago—"God save Merrie England and our King."